W9-DBS-865

A MAN CALLED RYKER

A MAN CALLED RYKER

Ray Hogan

NEW HANOVER COUNTY
PUBLIC LIBRARY
201 CHESTNUT STREET
WILMINGTON, N C 28401

Thorndike Press • Chivers Press
Thorndike, Maine USA   Bath, England

This Large Print edition is published by Thorndike Press, USA and by Chivers Press, England.

Published in 1999 in the U.S. by arrangement with Golden West Literary Agency.

Published in 1999 in the U.K. by arrangement with the author.

U.S. Hardcover   0-7862-2026-0 (Western Series Edition)
U.K. Hardcover   0-7540-3878-5 (Chivers Large Print)
U.K. Softcover   0-7540-3879-3 (Camden Large Print)

Copyright © 1971, by Ray Hogan

All rights reserved.

The text of this Large Print edition is unabridged.
Other aspects of the book may vary from the original edition.

Set in 16 pt. Plantin by Warren S. Doersam.

Printed in the United States on permanent paper.

British Library Cataloguing in Publication Data available

Library of Congress Cataloging in Publication Data

Hogan, Ray, 1908–
   A man called Ryker / Ray Hogan.
     p. cm.
   ISBN 0-7862-2026-0 (lg. print : hc : alk. paper)
   1. Large type books. I. Title.
   [PS3558.O3473M24   1999]
   813'.54—dc21   99-27124

A MAN CALLED RYKER

1

Jake Ryker was in the Lordsburg jail when the letter caught up with him.

It was the third of a ten day sentence for taking apart the Montezuma Saloon and for cracking a few heads during the process. The penalty had been a light one at that, the judge having taken into consideration that it was Ed Virden along with his younger brother, Chuck, and their dark-faced friend, Lenny Gault, who actually started it.

However, the jurist wasn't so generous that he felt Jake, six feet of redheaded toughness, should be excused for shattering half the mirrors in the place, smashing five tables and double that number of chairs, as well as tossing the blackjack dealer, who somehow got in the way, through a front window. In retrospect, Jake guessed it hadn't been necessary but, what the hell, at a time like that who keeps track?

The Virdens had been packing a grudge for him ever since Wichita, more than six months back, when he'd sided with a soldier they'd crowded into a fight. There'd been four of them then to the army boy's one.

Things changed when Jake evened up the odds a bit by declaring himself in; finally matters turned deadly when the fourth member of the Virden bunch — Tolly somebody — had gone for his gun. Jake Ryker beat him to the draw. That had started problems with the Virdens and Lenny Gault; they'd been dogging his tracks ever since.

But they were careful. Ryker's gun was known to be fast and sure, and while Wichita had created a festering sore, the three men were prudent enough to seek redress only when they felt they had Jake at a disadvantage. So far they'd had small success. Jake Ryker, despite the fact he had just passed his thirtieth birthday, carried the trail and town experience of double that number of years under his thatch of red, and never permitted himself to be caught off guard.

It was a trait that was as much a part of him as a leg or hand, for the life he led, that of drifter, paid gun, trail boss, gambler, shotgun rider and a dozen other similar vocations, had educated him early to

8

the fact that in such a world only the wary and the quick lived to ripe old ages. And while Jake never expected to reach the foot long beard and rocking chair category, there were still a few places he hoped to see, and things he'd like to do before he started bucking for the graveyard.

"This here letter," Town Marshal Borden said, studying the soiled and creased envelope thoughtfully, "sure has done some traveling around. Been clean up to Miles City, appears."

Jake, sprawled on the cell's hard cot, stirred disinterestedly. The drunk who'd shared the barred cubicle with him the first three days had been turned loose the night before and he'd finally managed to get some sleep.

"Can't think of nobody who'd be writing me," he said.

"How about some woman? Looks like a female's handwriting. You leave a little filly in a family way somewheres along the line?"

"Not as I can recollect," Ryker drawled and pulled himself to a sitting position. He yawned, stretched, scratched at the scruff of red beard making itself noticeable along his jaw. "You going to let me see it or you just aiming to stand there and guess about it?"

9

Borden shrugged, stepped in close to the bars and flipped the envelope to Jake. The tall rider grabbed for it, missed, knocked it under the cot on the opposite side of the cell. Mumbling a curse, he hunched forward, fished it out from under the narrow bench. Some previous occupant had forgotten a sock he noted while he was bent over — a black one with the heel worn through.

Settling back, he slid a finger under the flap of the envelope, not bothering to ascertain the postmarks under the smudges, and removed the sheet of lined and folded paper.

"From Callie," he said, glancing at the waiting marshal. "My brother Tom's wife."

The lawman's expectant face dropped, reflected keen disappointment. "Family, eh?" he said grudgingly. "Where they live?"

"Got a ranch east of here. On the Pecos near Haystack Mountain. Pa started it a long time back. When he died he left it to Tom and me — only I never was much for nursing cows. Just let Tom take over — after he and Callie got married up — and moved on."

"What's it doing going to Miles City?"

"Was forwarded up there. Had a job on a ranch just outside of the town for a spell. Folks there sent it on down here knowing I figured to hang around for a time . . . Looks like it's been to quite a few places," Jake said, examining the face of the envelope.

Ryker fell silent, sat motionless, moody eyes on the floor, the still unread letter in his hands.

"Ain't you going to read it? Could be something mighty important."

Jake shrugged, straightened. "Anything Callie's got to say to me sure'd not be important, far as I'm concerned," he said and again leaned back against the bars of his cell. Unfolding the sheet a second time, he began to decipher the cramped writing.

Dear Jacob:

I'm sending you this letter and hoping it will find you somewheres. Your brother Tom has been hurt. He'll never walk again the doctors tell us. He was thrown from a horse.

I can't run the ranch by myself and things are getting worse, especially the rustling. I think you ought to come home and do your share. Lord knows Tom has always done his. It's time you settled down.

Your sister-in-law,
Callie Ryker

11

A nice, friendly letter, Jake thought, folding the sheet — with about the same depth of affection and warmth a money lender would exhibit when he foreclosed on a one-legged widow. But that was Callie's way. She was right, however. If Tom had been made a cripple it was up to him to do something about it.

He swore softly. It was a hell of a thing to consider; ranching. Being tied down to raising cattle and having Callie looking over his shoulder griping and criticizing and bitching at him all day long. But he guessed there was no way around it. He'd have to ride over and see Tom and at least talk about it.

Rising, he moved to the front of his cell. Borden had moved away and now stood in the doorway of the building soaking up a little of the cooling breeze that was drifting in from the Gila to the north. It was hot for August, hotter than usual.

"Marshal, like for you to read this."

The lawman turned, sauntered lazily back to the cell block, extended his hand.

"Why? It got something to do with me?"

"Reckon so. Need to get out of here — now."

The older man brushed Ryker with a speculative glance, dropped his eyes to the

12

letter. He read slowly, laboriously, his lips moving with each word. Finished, he passed it back to Jake.

"Reason you're in here's because you didn't have the cash to pay your fine. Can't expect me to just up and turn you loose on account of a letter."

"Be the way to collect that fine. I get to the ranch I'll send the twenty-five dollars first off."

The lawman clawed at his chin. "Something to that, maybe. Your paying off, I mean. Costing the town a plenty to keep you. How'll I know you'll send the money?"

"Because I'm telling you I will. Now, don't get me wrong, Marshal; I'd a hell of a lot rather stay right here in jail eating three squares a day and taking it easy, than go back to that ranch. But once in a while something turns up that a man plain has to do. That's what I'm looking in the face right now — something I've got to do. Anyway, you know where I'll be."

Borden continued his thoughtful consideration. "The judge ain't in town. Won't be back for another three, maybe four weeks. You figure you can have that money here before then?"

Jake said: "I'll put it on the first stage

13

headed this way."

The marshal turned, picked up the ring of keys on his desk. Moving back to the cell, he unlocked the door.

"I'm agreeing," he said, once again turning to his desk. "And I'm betting that you're a man who'll keep his word; otherwise I'm going to come looking for you." Opening a drawer, he pulled out Ryker's belt and holster, added to them the pistol which he'd placed in a different drawer.

"Word's something I've never gone back on yet," Ryker said, strapping on his gear. "Don't aim to start now." He paused, a stillness coming over him. "What happened to the Virdens and Gault?"

Borden shrugged. "Took off, I expect. While I was busy with you, they slipped out the back door of the Montezuma. Ain't seen them since." The lawman studied Ryker through narrowing eyes. "Why? You aiming to look them up?"

"Not specially. Just hoping they've had enough. Where'd you put my horse?"

"Gabaldon's stable. Tell Chico I'll settle with him later."

Jake started for the door, hesitated again. He extended his hand. "Obliged to you, Borden."

The lawman clasped Ryker's hand in his

14

own, nodded curtly. "Just hoping you'll stay obliged."

"Don't fret over it, you'll get your money," Jake said and stepped through the doorway into the brilliant sunlight.

He swung his glance up and down the street, located Gabaldon's livery barn at the lower end. Immediately he headed for it, walking in the short, mincing way of a man who detested that mode of travel.

Gabaldon frowned when he stated his desire, glanced toward the jail. Borden evidently gave the stableman a confirming wave, for he turned immediately, headed back into the runway until he came to the stall quartering Ryker's sorrel.

"This is the one, *señor?*" he asked in heavily accented English.

Jake nodded. Moving to the separating partition upon which his gear had been racked, he saddled and bridled the sorrel, made him ready for the ride. That done, he unhooked his canteen, filled it from the water bucket outside the office door. He had a fair amount of trail grub in his saddlebags — enough he figured. There would be ranches and a few small towns along the way; he'd depend on them for meals.

Taking the sorrel's headstall in hand, he backed the gelding into the runway, swung

15

him about and moved to the doorway. In the better light he ran his eye over the horse, nodded appreciatively to Gabaldon, lounging now against the wall sucking at a thin, brown cigarette.

"You took good care of him."

"A fine animal," the stableman said, shifting his shoulders. Abruptly a frown covered his dark features. He straightened slowly. "*Amigo* — those men —"

Ed Virden's shout cut into Chico Gabaldon's words. "Come on out, Mister Gunslinger! This here's one time you ain't dodging me!"

11

Jake Ryker became a nerveless figure in the half-light of the stable. He looked beyond the sorrel's head. Ed Virden, Chuck and the cold-eyed Lenny Gault were in the shadowy rectangle of the passageway lying between the two buildings directly opposite. They could see him easily but were barely visible to him. He sighed heavily. He'd hoped they'd given it up.

"Ryker — you hear me?"

Jake scanned the area of the street fronting Gabaldon's. There was no cover of any sort. If he tried to make a run for it, they'd have him cold.

"I hear you."

"What's holding you back, Ryker? It'll be just you and me. The boys'll stay out of it."

Jake reached for the sorrel's reins. He glanced to Chico Gabaldon standing rigidly against the wall just inside the livery stable's entrance.

"There a back door to this place?"

"The end of the runway, to the left. You

will not face them?"

"No sense to it — and I've got enough trouble with the marshal."

"You coming out, Ryker?"

Jake turned his attention back upon the dim figures in the passageway. "Forget it, Ed. You've got no call to —"

"Forget — hell!" Virden shouted. "Had me a hunch you was a four-flushing sonofabitch when the chips were down. Giving you one more chance. You don't come out, then I'm coming in after you."

"Let it drop, Virden. I'm not —"

The blast of Ed Virden's pistol drowned Ryker's words. The lean rider sprinted into the street, crouched low, triggering his weapon as he came. His first bullet struck Chico Gabaldon, broke the stableman's arm. The second caught the sorrel in the head, killing the big horse instantly.

As the third bullet plucked at Ryker's sleeve, he dropped to one knee, coolly pressed off a shot. Ed Virden paused in mid-stride. A yell ripped from his throat, and then, throwing both arms wide, he fell forward into the dust.

Ryker, not moving, snapped a bullet into the ground a stride ahead of Gault, another at Chuck Virden's feet as they charged from the passageway. Both

18

hauled up short.

"Both of you — drop your irons!"

The two complied slowly. Men were now yelling in the street, and Jake could hear someone approaching at a run. The marshal, he guessed, and groaned quietly. He'd be lucky if he didn't wind up in a cell again.

"Now — back off!"

Virden and Gault began to move away. Ryker swung a glance to Gabaldon. The stableman was sitting in the doorway to his office. There was a dazed look on his face, and he was moaning softly as he clutched his arm.

"You hit bad?"

"The arm, *señor*. It is broke, I fear. And I bleed."

"I'll get you the doc —"

"Ryker — you still in there?"

It was Borden's angry voice.

"Come ahead, Marshal," Jake called back. "Somebody get the doc. Gabaldon's been hit."

A cry went up in the street for Vipperman, the local physician. Immediately after, Borden's distinct, nasal voice cut across the hush, pinning.

"You two — keep standing right there with your hands up. I got business with

19

you soon as I take care of what's there in the barn. Some of you men tote the dead one over to Vipperman's office. Ryker?"

Jake, kneeling beside the sorrel, loosening the cinch, glanced up. The lawman was standing just outside the wide doorway, a double-barreled shotgun in his hands. Beyond him onlookers were venturing closer with cautious steps, not certain yet that it was safe.

"You been shot?"

"No, I was lucky," Ryker replied. "He got Gabaldon in the arm. Killed my horse. Wasn't much else I could do, Marshal, but cut him down. Virden was throwing lead like he'd gone looney."

The lawman cradled his weapon. "No, suppose not. Reckon I ought to feel good there wasn't three, four others hurt by such crazy shooting . . . In there, Doc," he added as a second figure hurried into the doorway. "It's Chico."

A small, balding man, coatless, green garters pinning back his sleeves, bustled into the runway. He touched Ryker with curious, impersonal eyes, crossed to the stableman and hunched down beside him.

Ryker, the saddle free, turned his attention to the sorrel's bridle. "This mean I'm back in the jug?"

Borden glanced to the street. Ed Virden's body had been removed. Two or three volunteers were standing near the dead man's companions as if keeping them in hand until the lawman could take charge.

"Naw, reckon not," he said. "Even a gunslinger's got a right to defend himself — only I wish to God you jaspers'd stay away from my town and do your calling out somewheres else."

"Was trying to dodge him," Ryker said. "Didn't get the chance."

"Sure, sure! I can just see Jake Ryker ducking a shootout, especially with somebody he's had trouble with, just like I can see my grandma climbing to the moon."

"Es verdad," Gabaldon spoke up from the doorstep. "It is the truth, Marshal. He asked for the back way from my building. But that crazy one he start to come — shooting —"

Borden grunted. "Expect he wasn't ducking out. He was just aiming to circle around, get a better crack at Virden."

Ryker straightened up, eyed the lawman coldly. "I was leaving. Makes no difference to me whether you believe it or not."

Borden studied the redhead's stilled features. Somewhere in the settlement a

21

lonely bell was ringing, tolling in slow, measured beats. Finally the lawman shrugged.

"Maybe so. Well, I ain't stopping you. Sooner you're gone, better I'll like it."

"No horse."

Borden swore deeply, swung to Gabaldon, now rising unsteadily with the aid of the physician.

"Chico, man needs something to ride. I'll see he sends you the money for it."

Gabaldon waved a limp hand toward the rear of the stable. "A chestnut is back there. It wears my brand. For fifty dollars —"

"Fifty dollars —" Ryker began, frowning, and then his jaw snapped shut. He'd take the horse at any price just to get out of town while luck was still with him.

"It's a deal," he said. "Be needing a bill of sale."

"When the money is returned the paper will be sent," Gabaldon replied, moving into the runway with Vipperman supporting him.

"No good. Have to get it now."

"It'll be all right," Borden said. "The horse's got his brand. If he don't holler about it, who's going to question your riding it?"

22

"Somebody who knows him and his brand."

The lawman rubbed angrily at his neck. "Goddammit, all right! I'll give you a note saying you ain't no horse thief. That ease your mind?"

"It'll do," Ryker said, pulling the saddle from the dead sorrel. Gathering up the bridle and blanket, he headed for the back of the stable.

He found the chestnut, looked him over casually in the half-dark and felt better about the steep price. Throwing on his gear, he led the horse into the runway, halted. A dozen or more men were gathered in the stable's entrance talking to the marshal. The lawman saw him, broke away and came forward, a paper in his hand.

"This here'll get you by," he said, stuffing the folded sheet into Ryker's shirt pocket. "Says you're riding the animal with my authority. Anybody wanting to know why is to get in touch with me."

Jake nodded. "Obliged to you again, Marshal."

The lawman turned his head aside, spat. "Best way you can oblige me is to get the hell out of my town, and stay out. Trouble comes hunting you, Ryker, same as flies go after sugar. And use Gabaldon's back door

— I'd as soon you'd not go riding down the street. Could be Virden's got some more relations and friends hanging around aching to take a potshot at you."

Ryker nodded genially. "Sure thing," he said, wheeling the chestnut around. "So long."

III

Five days later, trail worn, gaunt, his neglected whiskers itching, with sweaty and dust-clogged beard, Jake Ryker pulled to a stop on the crest of a fair sized hill west of the Pecos and looked to the land across the winding strip of shining silver.

This was Ryker range — his actually, or at least half his; forty thousand acres, most of it good grass, with year around water, plenty of trees for shade, plus winters that were always mild and summers that usually were not too hot. All in all it was a fine place on which to raise beef, to become a cattleman.

The thought of such did not stir Jake Ryker. He was far more interested in the nearby crisscrossing trails and the places to which they led: Mexico, the lower end of Texas to the south, Fort Worth, Abilene, Wichita, Dodge City, the Indian Nations to the east; in the north the Colorado hills, and beyond them Wyoming, Montana and the Dakotas. And to the west the new territory of Arizona, Nevada, California with

25

its Gold Coast and wide open, hell-roaring San Francisco.

A man was a fool to tie himself down to a piece of land, he thought morosely, eyes drifting aimlessly across the gray green sea of grass. Late summer was like this; the hot sun altered the color of the growth from emerald to sage. And it hadn't been a wet spring. The Pecos, always low at this time of year, looked below normal.

He sighed, realizing that the lack or the surplus of water was to become one of his problems — if he stayed on. It seemed to Jake that every cattleman he knew was always worrying about something — the weather, disease, the market, rustlers . . .

Rustlers! Callie had mentioned something about rustlers in her letter. Evidently they were suffering heavy losses at the hands of cattle thieves. He could see how it could be a problem for the Circle R — too small to support a large crew; it was hard to control rustling when you were short of riders.

Something else he'd have to shoulder, he thought, and touching the chestnut with his rowels he rode down the hill. The gelding had been a good buy after all; he'd withstood the hard trip across New Mexico well. Maybe he wasn't the fastest

26

animal on four legs but he had plenty of bottom, could stay in there and work the whole day through.

Ryker cut down for the river on a long slant, pointing for a place where he had previously forded. He was still well below Circle R's buildings which were not visible to him because of the land's rolling contours. He should arrive there around midday, right at dinnertime. He grinned at that realization. Callie would have some pointed remark to make on that.

Well, she was the one who'd written the letter. His coming was her idea, and he'd never bothered them but once. That was when he needed a hundred dollars to help a friend in trouble. It hadn't seemed much to ask for. What the hell, he was half-owner of the place and had never taken a penny of its profits! A lousy hundred wasn't much interest to draw for his half-ownership. He smiled wryly, scratched at his beard. He needed another seventy-five to pay off Borden and Chico Gabaldon. Callie would holler to beat hell when she heard about that.

He reached the banks of the Pecos, followed along its grassy edge to where it sloped down to the water. The chestnut hesitated, ears pricking. Jake spurred the

27

big horse gently, and he moved out into the flowing stream, lower even than it had looked from the crest of the hill.

Gaining the opposite shore, Ryker guided the gelding up through a thick stand of nodding sunflowers onto solid footing, and moved into the long band of trees that grew along the river's east bank. Shortly he was in their cooling midst, enjoying the leafy shield from the hot sun.

A cottontail scooted out from under the chestnut's hooves, bobbed off at top speed to disappear into the low brush between the tree trunks. Somewhere a dove was cooing plaintively while a jay scolded impatiently.

All about Ryker was the warm, moist smell of the soil, of saw oats, wild hay, and of the red and white flowered beard plants that grew in such profusion in the sunny places. He'd all but forgotten about them, recalled then how as a child he'd often walked through the beds, deliberately crushing the stalks with his feet to release the musky scent.

That was a long time ago, twenty years or more, and since then things had changed greatly. The memory of his early life was something of a blur and there was little he could accurately recall; his ma, his pa, Tom, the bleakness of their existence; and he never forgot the wishful little ditty his father was forever humming: *come some day, the great day, I'll be rich and riding a tall horse, setting high on a fine saddle.*

But the time had never come, only bad years and a few good ones, and then there was the spring when his ma had died, and a year later when pa had followed . . . That was the knife that slashed the final tie for Jake — the passing of John Ryker. He'd managed to get along with Tom up till then for the sake of his parents, even with Callie who had become a member of the family just after his mother had died.

The day they laid Big John beside his wife on the slope east of the house, where they could look out over the land they'd loved and labored over for so long, however, was the day Jake Ryker made up his mind to get out. And he did, taking his leave before that same sun had set. Twice since then he had seen Tom and Callie. *Twice too often.* That's what it had amounted to, and he'd sworn never to return again, but here he was riding across Circle R range on the way to . . .

Ryker pulled up short. A distance ahead in a small clearing a half a dozen riders had gathered. A seventh man, hands tied

29

behind his back and astride a lean, spotted horse, was halted beneath the extended limb of a broadly spreading tree. There was a rope around his neck and one of the riders was endeavoring to throw the loose end of it over the horizontal limb.

Jake's mouth hardened. He'd seen enough of mob justice to know that it ordinarily was wrong, that the victim usually turned out to be innocent of the crime he was being made to pay the penalty for. Regardless, rope law was not the kind any man should adhere to.

Drawing his forty-five, he spurred the chestnut into a fast lope down the dappled lanes between the cottonwoods. Halfway to the clearing he fired a shot into the heavily leafed tree overshadowing the men, releasing a shower of green fragments.

Startled, the riders wheeled hurriedly, angrily. One reached for the weapon on his hip. Ryker snapped a warning bullet at him, froze his arm to his side.

"All of you — hold off!" he shouted, and racing up brought the chestnut to a stiff-legged halt.

30

IV

The men on the ground surveyed Ryker coldly. The rider with the rope about his neck heaved an audible sigh.

"I'm thanking you, Jake."

Ryker's brows drew together. Keeping his gun drifting back and forth over the small crowd, he swung off the saddle slowly, squinted at the near victim. Nat Clover — they'd ridden shotgun together for the old Nebraska-Kansas Stage Line three or four years back, had once been fairly close friends. Then he'd quit the company and moved on. Later he'd heard that Clover had cut loose, too.

"You about to pay for your evil ways, Nat?"

"All a mistake. I —"

"Mistake, hell!" An old puncher somewhere in his sixties took a quick step forward. His small, dark eyes snapped angrily. "We caught this here jasper cold — the damned rustler! Mister, you're horning in on something that sure ain't none of your business."

"Maybe," Jake replied quietly.

"We got proof," the man beside the old puncher said. He was well up in years, also, had straw-colored hair and a nose that had been flattened against his ruddy face. "You disbelieve us, then you just take yourself a gander at that butchered steer a laying over in that coulee."

"I'll take your word for it," Ryker said, and shifted his attention back to Clover. "What about it?"

The man on the spotted horse shrugged. "They's a steer over there, sure enough, only it wasn't me that butchered him. Was riding through here heading for Fort Worth. Heard somebody take off real suddenlike through the brush, so I cut in to have a look. Seen that steer a laying there. Throat'd been cut.

"Was just a setting there looking at him and wondering when this bunch snuck in on me, holding iron. Next thing I knew I was waiting to get my neck stretched . . . You mind untying my hands, Jake? Makes me real nervous to think what'll happen if this jughead I'm forking takes a notion to leave."

Ryker, circling the glowering punchers, moved to Clover's side. Taking his belt knife from its leather sheath, he sliced

32

through the cords that bound the man's wrists. Jaw set, he faced the others.

"You aimed to hang a man on that kind of evidence?"

"Was a plenty, far as we could see," the older puncher said. "We been losing us a lot of beef —"

"Nothing in that proves he had anything to do with it."

"That butchered steer, reckon it's proof."

"Proves somebody did some butchering, but not that it was him. You look to see if he had a bloody knife on him? There any spots on his clothes, his boots? A man that takes it on himself to carve up a live steer has got one hell of a job on his hands, and he'd sure get a lot of blood on himself."

The two elderly men exchanged glances, swung their attention to the remaining members of their party. All were considerably younger.

"Well, maybe we was going at it a mite hasty like. But seeing that steer, and him being there —"

"Good and handy," Ryker cut in sardonically.

"Yeh, reckon that was it, but —"

Jake heard a thud behind him, looked over his shoulder. Nat Clover had removed

33

the rope from his neck, thrown it to the ground.

"Close," he muttered, massaging his throat. "Too goddam close." He turned his pale eyes to Ryker. "Sure beholden to you for that one, partner. Now, maybe I'd best do me some settling up with these rope happy holy rollers. Which one of you's got my cutter?"

One of the younger punchers pulled out the pistol he'd thrust under his waistband. "Reckon I got it," he muttered and handed it, butt forward, to Clover. He faced Ryker squarely, frowned. "You making us let him go?"

"Not making you do anything except forget lynching him. You figure you've got proof enough to take him to a sheriff or a marshal, go right ahead. I won't stop you. I'm just dead set against your using a rope on him."

The young rider glanced uncertainly at his friends. They would all be Circle R cowhands, Jake guessed. He grinned faintly, thinking of Tom's reaction when word of what had taken place reached his ears. And Callie's.

"Well, I guess we ain't got no surefire proof, leastwise none we could talk to the law about. Ain't nothing to do but let him

34

go." It was one of the older men, the one who had spoken up first. He raised a bony finger, leveled it at Clover. "But you'd best remember this; this here's Circle R range you're a trespassing on, and strangers ain't welcome on it! If you're smart, you'll stay off 'cause next time maybe you won't be so lucky."

Nat Clover's dark face was cold, expressionless. He settled back on his heels as his shoulders hunched slightly. Jake, seeing all the old signs, shook his head and stepped in front of the man.

"Let it go, Nat. These boys are only doing their jobs."

The squat man's features did not change. "Nobody horses me around the way they did, throws a rope about my neck and gets away with it."

"Let it go," Ryker said again, quietly.

Clover turned his eyes to Jake. For a brief time their glances locked, and then he looked away, shrugged his thick shoulders.

"Sure, Jake, whatever you say."

"And about riding across this range. Might be smart to stick close to the river. Nobody'll fault you for being there."

"What I'll do. You headed east?"

"No, not right now."

The oldster with the straw hair shifted

35

from one foot to another, shoved his head forward. "You're mighty free telling folks what they can do on somebody else's property! Just who the hell are —"

"Who are you?" Ryker broke in.

"Me? Name's Vern Thatch, if it's any of your put in."

"Happens it is. Who're the rest?"

Thatch looked hard at Ryker for a long breath, brushed at the sweat gathered on his leathery brow. He seemed uncertain as to whether he should answer or not. Something in the tall redhead's manner brought him to a decision.

Jerking a thumb at the other older man, he said, "He's Ford, Wilbur Ford. Young one there with all the hair is Sam Neff. Next to him, that's Amos Quinn. The *vaquero* calls hisself Cristobal Sanchez. Last one with the fancy vest is Carl Delaney. Now, who might you be?"

"You all work for the Circle R, I take it?"

"You take it right, else we wouldn't be here."

"Makes sense," Jake said mildly. He swung about to Clover. "Expect you'll be riding on."

Clover, back in the saddle and settled, bobbed his head. "Reckon I will. You might as well throw in with me and come along. Hear things are mighty good around Fort Worth."

"Later maybe. Could change my mind."

Nat Clover nodded again. "Knowing you, I'll be waiting at the first town on the way," he said, and moved out. "Luck."

"Luck," Jake replied, a slight wistfulness in his tone. Fort Worth always was a good town.

"You ain't never got around to giving me a answer," Thatch pressed testily.

Jake pulled his attention away from Clover's departing figure. "Seems I haven't. Name's Ryker."

Thatch stared. The others stirred, glanced about. Wilbur Ford hawked, spat, clawed at his chin.

"You'd be that brother of Tom's I've heard him mention now and then."

"That's me, Jake Ryker. They sent me a letter quite a spell back. Chased me all over the country, finally caught up in Lordsburg." He broke it off there, seeing no point in going into further details regarding his presence there. "Tom any better?"

"No better'n nor worse'n he'll ever be. Got hisself busted up something awful by that horse."

"Callie said he'd been thrown. Never

37

said much else."

"You come to take over the place?" It was the youngster, Sam Neff. "If so, I reckon I'll just draw my time and move on."

Ryker's brows lifted. "Why?"

Neff shifted uncomfortably. "Was sort of high-handed, way you took up for that rustler. Tom and his missus sure ain't going to like it."

Jake's genial smile covered the edge to his words. "I don't give a goddam whether they do or not. Nat Clover's no rustler."

"You only got him saying that."

"Enough, far as I'm concerned. Known him for quite a spell. Been in a few tight spots together. He'd not lie to me, no more'n he'd rustle one steer. Maybe you're quitting because you don't like being caught in the wrong. I've seen a few cowhands that way — mostly young."

"No sense leaving," Ford said then. "Hell, we was all in on it. And if Mr. Ryker says that bird's all right, it's good enough for me." The old man reached out a gnarled hand. "I'm right proud to meet you, Mr. Ryker."

"Make it Jake," Ryker said, taking Ford's fingers into his own.

He went through the ritual of meeting

with each of the other riders. "This the whole crew?" he asked when it was done.

"The whole kit and kaboodle," Ford replied. "Ain't running much stock. Things ain't been so good, what with Tom all stove up and —"

"And the rustling going on," Thatch broke in.

"I was thinking about that," Jake said. "If you're the crew, who's looking after the herd? Be a real good time for rustlers to just help themselves."

Ford looked down in embarrassment. The others shuffled about nervously, turned away.

"Expect you're right, Mr. — uh — Jake," Wilbur mumbled. "Was a fool stunt, us all sashaying up here, but we allowed as how we had us a cow thief for certain." He placed his attention on the *vaquero* and the other younger men. "You boys get yourselves back to where the stock's grazing fast. Me and Vern'll rustle us up a bite to eat then spell you off 'til supper."

The riders moved off at once, going to their horses at a hurried, shambling gait, mounting quickly and whirling off as if anxious to be gone.

Jake glanced at the remaining men. "Expect I'd best be riding on and tell Tom

39

and Callie I'm here. You headed for the ranch?"

Both nodded. "We been doing the night-hawking," Vern Thatch explained. "Reason we ain't pounding leather along with the other boys. Fact is, we ought to be sleeping right now, but it was so danged hot we couldn't do it. So we rode out to see how things was. Got here just as the boys collared that rus— that friend of your'n."

"I see," Jake said, swinging to the saddle. The four Circle R punchers were just topping out a ridge a quarter mile distant. Nat Clover had long since dropped from sight. "All of you been with Tom for a long time?"

Thatch paused as he prepared to mount. "Not too long. Me and Will've been here the longest, excepting for old Cocinero — he's the Mex cook."

"I recollect him," Jake said, cutting the chestnut about. "Was here when I left."

"Expect he was doing the cooking even before your pa died."

"He was," Ryker said, and urged the gelding into a lope.

He had no liking for what lay ahead at the ranch, but the sooner he got there, the quicker he'd get the meeting with Tom and Callie over with.

V

The barn and the main house had been enlarged. The crew's quarters and the lesser sheds looked just the same. There were two new corrals, and the big cottonwoods that spread their welcome shade over all were even larger than he had remembered.

Otherwise, there was little change; that same bleak, colorless look he'd expected. As bound by drudgery as his mother had been, even she had found time to encourage a few wild flowers around the yard in an effort to dispel the desolation; you'd think Callie could have done the same.

He saw her then. She was standing in the doorway of the main house, hands on hips, streaked, blonde hair untidy and straggling down about her face, which had the shine of sweat upon it. She was wearing a faded, gray dress with a square-hemmed apron, one corner of which had been folded up and tucked under the waist tie for some reason.

Callie Ryker had never been a beautiful

41

woman, but she had been attractive in a severe sort of way. She could still be if she'd take the time to fix herself up a bit. That sleazy, gray dress for instance.

"So you finally got here."

She spoke even before he pulled his horse to a stop at the hitchrack. He stared at her wordlessly, temper, as always, stirring within him. It would never change, he supposed, the hostility and antagonism she felt for him.

"Letter was a long time catching up," he said and swung from the saddle.

"Just what I thought. If you'd ever take a job somewheres, stay with it instead of running off tramping around —"

"Now, Callie," he cut in softly, firmly, shaking his head. "How's Tom?"

Callie Ryker shrugged, pushed open the screen and stepped out onto the porch. The door banged shut, dislodged a cloud of powdery dust that drifted slowly to the floor.

"The same."

Jake wound the chestnut's leathers around the crossbar started for the gallery. Behind him Thatch and Will Ford had curved off to the bunkhouse, were dismounting in that stiff-jointed way of men grown too old for the saddle.

42

"Was real sorry to hear about the accident," Jake said halting, one foot in the yard, the other on the edge of the porch.

Callie's shoulders moved again. "Would have to happen to *him*," she said in an exasperated tone, and let her words hang.

Jake gave her a tight grin. "Instead of to some no-good saddle bum like me," he finished. "Want to see him."

"He's sleeping. Had a bad night. You'll have to wait an hour or two." She paused, considered him warily. "You here to stay or are you just passing through?" The edge to her voice was razor sharp.

"Depends. Not keen about it but if I'm needed and it can be worked out, reckon I will. Either way it'll cost you seventy-five dollars, my coming here. Owe for my horse and — and another debt."

She turned, eyes flaring and sharp, gave him a long look, and then came half about, stared out over the sun-baked hardpan to the range beyond. The weariness, the worn hopelessness of her were reflected in the slack, lined planes of her face, the lassitude that gripped her. In spite of himself, Jake Ryker felt a stirring of pity for the woman.

"Wish't I could believe that, that you'd help."

"Mean what I've already said, but you

43

know what the problem's always been."

"Callie? Who's out there?"

At the call from inside the house, she turned slowly to the door. "It's Jake. He's got here."

"Jake! Bring him in here."

Ryker stepped up onto the porch, crossed over and entered the house without waiting for her to relay the request. Moving through the familiar kitchen, now a sort of sitting room since the cook handled all meal preparations in an adjacent cook shack, he stepped into the room that had been his parents' sleeping quarters. The small square that he and Tom had occupied lay off the opposite wall.

He moved to the head of the bed, masking the shock he felt at sight of the frail, broken man, once tall and dark and powerful enough to upend a thousand pound steer, extended his hand.

"Good to see you again, Tom."

The older Ryker responded limply. "Same here, kid. Wasn't sure you'd come when Callie decided she'd best write you."

Jake shook his head. "Hell, you ought've known I would. Just sorry it took so long. Things are looking kind of bad, I hear."

Tom nodded. Reaching back he grasped the iron uprights of the bed's headpiece,

44

drew himself to a sitting position. Jake leaned forward to assist, drew back when his brother frowned.

"Only a few things I can do for myself. This is one of them. Callie tell you about all our troubles?"

"Some," Jake answered sitting down on the edge of the hard mattress. "Ran into your crew out on the range. Were about to string up a fellow I know for rustling."

"About to?"

"I stopped them. Man wasn't guilty."

Tom Ryker's drawn face settled into a grimness. "They must've had proof of some kind."

"They found him near a butchered steer, figured he did it."

"Sounds to me pretty much like he might have."

Jake said, "No, I know the man. He's no rustler. Anyway, you don't lynch somebody on evidence like that. Seen too many mistakes made along those lines."

"What happened to this — this friend of yours?"

"Turned him loose, sent him on his way."

Tom Ryker's jaw clicked shut. "Goddammit all to hell, Jake! Here we're being stole blind and you —"

45

"He's not the man you're looking for," Jake said stubbornly. "I know Nat Clover from times back and —"

"You know! Jesus God, the kind you run with, I —"

Jake Ryker drew himself up slowly. A tautness had slipped into him, now held him in a firm grasp.

"It'll never change will it, Tom? Just no way on this earth for you to see me except as the no-account kid brother who doesn't have a lick of sense."

"Hell, I'm sorry," the older Ryker said after a pause. "Guess this being laid up has done something to me."

"No, that's not it and you know it. It was this way before. The years haven't changed a thing."

"Why shouldn't he feel that way?" Callie said from the doorway. "You ever do anything to prove him wrong?"

"Maybe not to your way of thinking," Jake said without turning. "But everybody doesn't look at things the same as you do. Lots of folks figure other things are important, things you think are nothing."

"Trail bums, saloon swampers, dance hall girls, gamblers!" Callie ground out the words as if they were epithets. "They're the kind of people you're talking about!"

46

"Maybe, and there's a few others, too. But no matter. It's something we'll never see eye to eye on."

"You can be certain of that!" Callie snapped. "And if you think for one minute I —"

"Now, wait," Tom Ryker cut in, raising a limp hand. "We're going at this all wrong. No use us ranting at Jake. What's been is past. It's over and done with. We got no call to go raking him over the coals just because he ain't done the way we figure he ought —"

Jake's shoulders lifted, settled resignedly. "See? Just what I'm talking about. But you're dead right about one thing; there's no point hashing over the past because I plain won't listen to it. That clear?"

Tom shrugged his thin shoulders, nodded. Jake swung his curt gaze to Callie. She looked away, her answer grudging but there, nevertheless.

"Then that's settled. Way I've lived my life is my business, and from here on I don't see that there's any need to complain, either one of you. I could have been ragging you regularly for my half-share of everything this place has made —"

"Made?" Callie interrupted. "We haven't made a dollar since the day Tom got hurt!"

47

"You had plenty of good years before that when you were getting the benefit of my half — but don't get me wrong. I'm not complaining. You were doing the work, you were entitled to all you made and stashed away."

"Which was damned little," Tom said bitterly. "And that's most gone now, what with all the doctors and all the medicines. They even brought some specialist down here all the way from Albuquerque. Cost like hell. And then me just laying here with the place going to pot."

Jake brushed at the sweat on his face, considered deeply. It wasn't what he wanted but there are times when a man is forced to accept a duty.

"I'm here to stop that," he said finally, coming to a decision. "But I'll do it my way. I want that understood between us right now. I'll run this ranch the way I think best."

"And run it straight into the ground!" Callie said acidly.

Jake Ryker folded his arms across his chest, jutted his bearded chin at her and met her eye to eye. "Then why the hell did you send for me if you think that's what I'd do?"

Her gaze wavered, broke, shifted to the

48

open window. A light breeze was drifting in, fanning the lace curtains, relieving, to some extent, the breathless heat.

"Nothing else I could think of . . . I — I wanted you to come — help."

"To come take orders from you, that's what you mean, isn't it?" Jake demanded. "Can see that now. Ought've had sense enough to see it sooner, but I was thinking about Tom. Well, it won't work."

The elder Ryker pulled himself a bit higher on the bed. His sallow face showed alarm. "Won't work? That mean you —"

"Means just what I said before. If I'm to take over this ranch, I'll take it over all the way, bottle, barrel and bung starter."

"You don't even know —"

"I'll call the shots, all of them, and do the deciding and the planning. You're in no shape to. Face up to it, Tom, no man ever yet run a ranch from a bedstead or a rocking chair."

"Maybe not, but that's no reason why I can't be in on the decisions of what's to be done."

"There's plenty of reasons. The biggest one being that we don't agree on anything. We never have, expect we never will."

Both Callie and Tom were silent, admitting to themselves, no doubt, the truth of the statement. Finally the woman stirred.

"Well, don't suppose things can get much worse than they are. Either way seems we're bound to go broke and lose everything."

"We might," Jake admitted, "but I don't figure it that way. One thing you maybe don't know. All this time you've had me pegged for running around the country drinking and raising hell and getting into shooting scrapes and the like is not exactly true.

"Held a few jobs then, some of them pretty good ones, in fact. Was the ramrod for a spread up Wyoming way once, one so big you could lose this cabbage patch on its south range. I'm no greenhorn when it comes to running a spread and handling cattle. Few other times, too, but there's no need going into it."

Tom studied him silently for a long minute when he finished, finally shifted his dull eyes to Callie. "Can't see as we've got a choice, and maybe we ought to be grateful."

"Don't want you to be grateful. Just want you to savvy now that if I'm to take over, it's to be with no halter ropes hanging from my neck. There's to be no cutting in, no interfering."

50

Tom nodded wearily. "We're agreeing. You'll run the place. Could be Callie and me'll move into town, get us a little house."

Callie flung her husband a surprised look. "Leave here — everything — to him?"

"Would be a good idea," Jake said approvingly. "Get you away from a lot of stewing and fretting."

"Just something we can think about," Tom said, continuing to ignore Callie. "What do you say?"

Jake was silent briefly, then bobbed his head. "Guess we can say it's settled. I'll take hold, get things running right. First off, I've got to put a stop to the rustling that's going on."

"No," Tom cut in flatly, "first off you're to go after some cattle I agreed to buy."

Jake Ryker's jaw tightened. Anger flashed in his eyes, and then a sort of desperation came over him. He gave his brother a long, straight look, shrugged . . . He should have known it would be this way.

"The hell with it," he said with finality, and turned for the door.

VI

"Now wait a damn minute."

At Tom's anxious protest Jake Ryker never slowed but continued on for the doorway. Callie, standing squarely before him, did not stir, simply watched him with her cold eyes.

"No use. It won't work. Neither one of you'll let it," he said. "Saw a sample of that right then."

Callie bristled at once. "You think it'll be easy for him to sit back and let you or anybody else take over everything he's worked like a dog all these years to build?"

Jake, forced to halt, studied her set features. "You think it'll be easy for me to give up the kind of living I'm used to — and enjoy? Anyway, I think he and you had better cotton to the idea quick or there won't be anything left of the Circle R for me or anybody else to take over."

"Never meant that to sound the way it came out," Tom said gruffly. "Only with everything piling up the way it is and going sour, I —"

"Which will be my worry, not yours."

Callie drew aside, placed her shoulders against the wall adjacent to the doorway. The bitterness that possessed her was like a mask, flattening her features, pocketing her eyes in deep, dark circles.

"He's right Tom," she admitted, defeated. "We've got no choice. Either we let him run it his way or we lose everything we've got. Far as I can see the chances are about even."

Jake gave her a side look. "Thanks for the vote of confidence," he said dryly. "Expect the best thing you can do is find yourself a foreman to run things, let him handle your troubles and fight off the rustlers."

"Dammit, said I was sorry," Tom snapped irritably. "What more you want? And there ain't no sense in you flying off the handle. Thought by now you'd have outgrown that."

"Never seem to have the problem except when I'm around you," Ryker replied evenly. "You still think I'm ten years old, and until you get that out of your head, I can't see's there's any use trying to get along."

"Good God!" Tom shouted, abruptly furious. "What do you want me to do, get down on my knees and beg?"

"Nope," Jake said quietly, turning completely about to face his brother. "Just want you to stay out of my hair. It's the only way I can help. And I'll do a job for you until I can find a good man to hire on as foreman."

"Foreman? You mean you won't stay on permanent?"

"No sense in trying. Be no satisfying you and Callie long as you're on the place. But I'll be here until I can locate the right man."

Callie's eyes held a sullen glow. Her lips moved to shape a quick, caustic remark, and then she thought better of it, and the words were never spoken.

Tom Ryker stirred, settled back resignedly. "All right, Jake, all right. Let's quit ragging it over. You take hold, run the Circle R the way you think best. Callie and me'll stay out of your way, have nothing to do with it. Leastwise we will after you've got back with the cattle I've bought."

"Bought?"

"What I was telling you. Got to pick up two hundred head from Park Justin, over on the Texas Brazos. Can get them for ten dollars a throw if I — we'll take them now.

Next spring the same beef will bring double that price at the railhead."

Jake nodded his approval. "Sounds smart. Two hundred head all he'll let us have?"

"No, but it's all the cash we can spare."

"About all we've got, you mean," Callie corrected.

Tom Ryker said, "Yeah, guess that's closer to the truth. But that two hundred head, added to what we can afford to sell from our regular herd next spring — assuming we get the rustling stopped — will get us out of the hole and put us in pretty fair shape again."

"How much time've we got to pick up that stock?"

"Should've been there a month ago. Was no way I could make it, and nobody I could send."

"There's not many we want to trust with two thousand dollars in cash," Callie said pointedly.

"Including me, I suspect," Jake added, unable to withhold the comment.

Callie only sniffed. Tom said, "Don't mean I wouldn't trust Will Ford or Thatch. Both of them are as honest as the day is long, but you just don't unload that kind of responsibility on a man. Don't

55

see as there's any problem where you're concerned."

"A man packing that much cash has got himself a big problem!" Jake said. "Word slips out he's carrying that kind of money every owlhoot north of the Mexican border will be out to bushwhack him. Got to be a better way . . . How about a bank draft?"

"What bank? Closest one where you can get a draft is in El Paso. Riding that far is about as chancy as the trip to Justin's, maybe more so."

Jake Ryker gave that some thought, agreed. Then, "Whereabouts on the Brazos is Justin's spread?"

"Near Ben City. Good two hundred and fifty miles from here. Figured to take Sam Neff and the *vaquero* with me. Three can handle a herd that size."

"Best not to pull anybody off the range," Jake said. "Running the place shorthanded could lose us a lot of steers to the rustlers. Might cost us more'n we'd make on the two hundred."

"Hell, one man sure couldn't drive two hundred —"

"Wouldn't try. Best to pick up a couple of cowhands over there, hire them on for a month. What time is left when we got back

56

they could spend helping us clean out the rustlers."

"Cost money. I'm paying thirty a month and —"

"Cheap insurance," Jake said, dismissing what he considered petty arguing. "You got a letter or something from this Justin? Hate to ride that far and have him tell me there's no deal."

"Yeah, there's a letter, but you won't need it. Justin's in the business. Done some buying from him before."

"Best I take the letter anyway, just so's there'll be no changing of the price."

An eagerness had come over Tom Ryker. "Then — from the way you're talking — you're staying on?"

"Long enough to get things back in shape and find you a good man . . . I'll do that if we're understood there's to be no horning in and backbiting and getting in my way."

The elder Ryker bobbed his head. "It's understood. Want you to say it too, Callie."

The woman shrugged indifferently. "All right . . . I'll go get the money."

"No rush," Jake said, eyes narrowing cynically. "Maybe the saloons and gambling halls won't open until sundown."

A half-smile pulling at his lips, he glanced to Tom. His brother was studying him intently, almost with apprehension.

"Don't fret," Jake said then with a laugh. "The money'll be safe, safe as it is right here in this house. But I won't be needing it until morning. Aim to pull out around sunup."

Tom relaxed. "Good enough. Meanwhile, you'd best pile your belongings in the other bedroom, the one we used to sleep in."

"All the same to you, I'll throw in with the crew in the bunkhouse. Want to get a mite better acquainted with them. Travel light, anyway. Never pack much gear."

"How about trail grub and the like? You want Callie to tell Cocinero to fix you up?"

"I'll tell him," Jake said, making a point of it. "Just as soon as I can walk through that door and get to the kitchen. After that I'm calling the crew together, setting up a regular range watch, day and night, over the herd. Every man will be carrying a cocked Winchester, and nobody had better fall down on his job or he won't be working on this ranch."

"Now, Jake, they're all good men. You can't expect them to —"

"I'll be expecting plenty," Ryker said.

58

"Best they know that right off." Abruptly he grinned, passed through the doorway and struck for the back entrance. "See you around suppertime."

VII

The morning was a fine one, sweet and clear, before the day's heat began to lay its shimmering blanket across the land. Jake Ryker, astride the chestnut, followed the well-marked trail that would take him eventually to Park Justin's spread on the Brazos with the attentive appreciation of a man who loved and never tired of the grandeur and solitude of the vast countryside.

It would be a long, three day ride, one that could possibly be stretched to four; this depended on the big gelding's ability to stand up under the steady traveling Ryker expected to do. But the horse had pretty well proven itself on the trip from Lordsburg to the Circle R, and there should be no problem now.

But they had just started, and Jake guessed he should be more concerned about the money he was carrying — two thousand dollars in paper and gold pieces in a belt strapped around his middle. He swore softly. It was a lousy bit of bad luck. No man with any sense would tote that much cash about on his person. It was an open invitation to robbery and death if it leaked out which, somehow, such news always seemed to do. A lot of men had been shot out of the saddle for a tenth of that amount.

He'd taken every precaution possible to avoid the word being spread. Only Tom and Callie knew of it, thus he felt fairly secure at that end of the line. That Thatch and the other Circle R punchers would guess and speculate was unavoidable, but he expected to be far enough away from the Pecos country to be safe if they did spill a few hints.

Big thing necessary, he felt, was that he permit no inkling of it to escape him personally, and there was but one way to accomplish that; keep an ordinarily tight lip buttoned even tighter.

He glanced to the warming sun, now well above the horizon and beginning to climb into its curved canopy of flawless blue. It would be another hot one, he could see that — but then it was seldom the summer days weren't scorchers on the Staked Plains country. A man simply girded himself to face them, to accept the blistering heat, the sweat, the powdery dust and an occasional brush with Indians.

61

He shifted on the saddle. The horse was moving along at an easy lope covering the miles easily and efficiently. If he could hold to the pace, they would make it to Taladega, sprawled half in New Mexico, half in Texas, by nightfall with no difficulty. He could spend the night there quietly, get another early start the next morning.

Brushing at the sweat already gathered on his face, Ryker grinned wryly. He'd best be damned careful in Taladega. It was a wild, tough, wide-open town since its divided position made law enforcement practically an impossibility. It was a prevalent joke that a man committing a crime on one side of the street had but to cross over to the other to avoid the consequences of his act, so distinct was the lack of cooperation between the New Mexico and Texas law officers.

Thoughtful, Jake stared ahead into the building heat. If something happened and he lost the two thousand dollars through no fault of his own, he'd never be able to convince Callie and Tom of his innocence. They'd believe that he'd gambled it away, lent it to some worthless trail acquaintance, or through some act of carelessness while in the company of such friends, had

62

allowed it to slip through his fingers.

He wasn't about to let it happen — not under any circumstances short of being killed. It wasn't only that Tom and his wife needed a few mistaken impressions of him corrected — mainly that he was not a man capable of handling any task assigned him — but hell, when you came right down to boot heels, half of that money actually was his! And while that did not make the other half any less important, it did place a somewhat different premium upon its value.

But he'd have no trouble. He knew Taladega, was fully aware of its dangers and pitfalls and could easily avoid them. He'd be there for the one night only, anyway, and a man could hardly get himself in trouble just riding in, having a meal and maybe a drink, and then crawling into bed. He'd not even bother to look up the few friends he had there. Not that he didn't trust them, but it simply made good sense not to advertise his presence.

At noon he halted in a deep arroyo where an overhanging cedar cast a small pool of shade. He rested the chestnut for the better part of an hour, taking advantage of the break to eat a bit of the lunch old Cocinero, who had been pleased to see him again, had prepared. It was too hot to make coffee. He washed down the bread and meat with a swallow or two of water from his canteen. Afterward he gave the gelding a drink by soaking a rag and squeezing it dry into the horse's mouth. Then he rode on.

He met no one, saw no one in the distance. It was a glittering, baked land inhabited only by jackrabbits, snakes, a few horned larks and whip-tailed lizards, who were making a point of keeping out of the sun's direct rays.

Late in the day, with the smoke of Taladega hanging in a dirty gray smudge against the horizon, he did see a coyote, a lean, shaggy, starved looking brute that watched him from a safe distance with lowered head and yellow eyes.

And then, near sundown, he encountered two riders heading west, choosing to begin their journey across the flat in the cooler night hours. They were strangers, cattlemen from their appearance and tack. Both lifted their hands in the customary, reserved salutation of passing wayfarers unknown to each other but acquainted through the fact of being mutually engaged in traversing a lonely land.

Lamps were being lit when he reached

64

the edge of town and turned into its main street. Quite a number of horses were at the hitchracks, and he noted a good many rigs drawn up in the wagon yards. It occurred to him that the settlement was unusually busy, and then he realized it was Saturday, the customary time for ranchers and homesteaders to bring their families to town for shopping and for the cowhands who could get away to come in and slake their thirst for drink and companionship.

Riding slowly down the center of the wide lane, ankle-deep in loose dust that had not felt the kiss of rain in months, Ryker's glance cut back and forth. It had been a bit more than a year since he was last in Taladega; he noticed small change.

The LONE STAR SALOON & GAMBLING HALL . . . GIRLS, was still by far the largest, most active and best lighted edifice on the Texas side of the street. THE CATTLEMAN'S HOTEL, the ACE HIGH CAFE, THE EMPORIUM — GENL. MCHDS. FOR ALL were companion business firms still in operation, along with any number of small, hole-in-the-wall saloons and shops.

On the New Mexico side, it was the GOLD DOLLAR HOTEL with its connecting liquor, gambling and dancing facilities that dominated all other establishments. Ranged along with it were the competitors of the firms facing them in a row from the opposite bank: J. GRUNSFELD, THE HOME STORE; MISS EVE'S LADIES & CHILDRENS READY-TO-WEAR; GORDON'S GUN AND SADDLE SHOP; ESSLINGER'S GENT'S CLOTHING & BOOTS . . . All were familiar if fading signs to him.

There were many persons moving along the board sidewalks and loafing on the landings of the business concerns. Several were familiar to Jake but he was careful to return their glances with only a slight nod and did not slow the chestnut's walk, simply continued on until he came to the Gold Dollar. There he veered from the street into an alley that came in at right angles and led to the hotel's stable a short distance behind it.

Reaching the broad, squat structure, he came off the saddle stiffly, glad to be on solid ground after so many hours. Giving instructions to the hostler as to the gelding's care, he slung his saddlebags over his shoulder and made his way to the hostelry's back entrance.

Pulling open the door, he stepped into the narrow hallway. It was cool inside the building, shielded from the heat by two-foot thick adobe walls, and he felt a glow of anticipation when he visualized a night's sleep in the comfort of the hotel's interior.

Moving down the hall, he entered the lobby and crossed to the desk, ignoring the noisy clamor in the adjoining saloon, which was connected to the receiving part of the Gold Dollar by a wide archway. Thick, green portieres hung in the opening but as far as Jake knew, the heavy drapes had never been drawn.

"Need a room," he said to the waiting clerk.

The elderly man with a beet red face and wearing an eyeshade, bobbed his head. "Sure thing, Mr. Ryker," he said, and pushed a register and a stub of pencil to the front of the counter.

Jake studied the clerk briefly, guessed he was being remembered from his last stopover, and taking up the pencil, signed in.

"Be number five," the clerk said, reaching for a key. "Top of the stairs, to the left."

Ryker turned to the narrow flight of steps. Something crashed to the floor in the saloon and a woman's laugh pealed out above the shouts and cursing of a man and

67

the muffled rumble of general conversation.

Still ignoring the confusion, Jake continued mounting the steps slowly, wondering perhaps if he wouldn't have been better off to camp out on the flat; with the crowd that was packing Taladega that night, a man might find it hard to get any sleep.

"Knowed you'd show up!"

Ryker halted, arrested by the familiar voice. He turned half around, threw his glance back into the lobby. It was Nat Clover.

"Got me a room here, too," the squat man said, grinning broadly. "Soon's you stash your gear, come on down. I'll be waiting in the saloon."

VIII

Ryker muttered under his breath. It had been his hope to encounter no one he knew, that he could pass through the settlement unnoticed. He shrugged, decided then that it didn't really matter. As long as no one knew the details of his trip nothing could go wrong; to act suspicious would be a mistake. It would be best to simply go about things as usual.

"Figured you'd be about halfway to Fort Worth by now," he drawled, leaning against the wall.

"Ain't in no big rush, and it'll sure still be there when I show up . . . You eat yet?"

Jake watched the layers of smoke drifting from the saloon into the lobby and on toward the open doorway. "Nope. About the second thing I aim to do."

"Second? What's first — find yourself a woman?"

"No, wash off some of the dust . . . Go ahead, I'll meet you soon's I've cleaned up."

"Good enough. I'll be looking for you."

Jake resumed the short climb, gained the upper hallway and sought out his room. The quarters provided by the Gold Dollar were a notch better than average, being clean, cool and with furnishings that were fairly new. Fresh water was in the china pitcher on the washstand, and after stepping out of his clothes, he slopped a measure into the accompanying bowl and scrubbed himself down.

He felt better and buckling the money belt again around his lean middle, he snapped the loose dust from the shirt he'd been wearing, drew it on. He was carrying only one complete change of clothing and figured it was best to wait another few days before switching.

Dressed, he made his way to the saloon. Halting in the archway, he glanced about, nodded to several familiar faces, and then, spotting Clover at the blackjack table, crossed to join him.

"Luck's sure running fine," Nat said, grinning. "Ought to try your'n."

Jake had a few dollars in his pockets he'd brought along for expenses above the sum he was carrying for the cattle deal — and he did feel right. Nodding to the dealer, he entered the game. The cards fell favorably, and in less than a quarter hour he had won five times straight and accumulated a winning of twenty-five dollars or so.

The thought came to his mind then; with luck running for him, it might be wise to take a couple of hundred out of the cattle money, build it up to where he'd have some extra for expenses, or perhaps he'd do well enough to increase his capital and be in a position to buy more stock from Justin.

Such would be a big boost for Tom and the Circle R, he knew, toying with the thought. Showing up with fifty or a hundred more steers than expected would really open some eyes! And he was feeling right.

Jake Ryker shrugged. He'd be a damned fool to take a chance. Sometimes a man's luck changed so swiftly that he was broke before he knew it. Besides, he was beat from the long ride, and he was hungry.

Turning away, he said to Clover: "Think I'll get a bite to eat. You stay put while you're running hot. I'll meet up with you later."

"About time I was quitting, too," the scar-faced rider said, knuckling his bloodshot eyes. "Cards ain't falling like they was, and I'm ready for eating. Where'll we

71

go, the Ace High?"

"Still the best, I reckon. Cleanest for sure."

They crossed the gambling area, scarcely noting the adjoining room where a half a dozen garishly dressed women were performing lethargically on a small stage for an audience of two or three dozen men, and avoiding the lobby, entered the street. The Ace High restaurant lay on the Texas side, down a half a dozen doors.

Shouldering their way through the crowd milling aimlessly about in the shadowy light of store window lamps, they reached the cafe. The place was enjoying a good patronage, but they found an empty table near the back and sat down. The waitress, a young Mexican girl with coal black hair and very white teeth appeared at once and took their orders. She returned to the kitchen, walking with an exaggerated swinging of her well-curved hips.

"See you made up your mind to go to Fort Worth after all. Knowed when I mentioned it, there'd be no roping you down," Clover said as they settled back to await their meal. There had been little opportunity for general conversation back at the Gold Dollar's blackjack table.

"Not exactly where I'm headed," Jake

replied. "Only going far as the Brazos — Ben City."

"Ben City. Sort of recollect something special about it. What's there?"

"Only been there once myself. Not much more than a wide place in the road."

"Then why the hell do you want to fritter good time on a —"

"Little business I'm taking care of for my brother."

Nat Clover's mouth parted into a grin. "Sure! Recollect now what I'd heard about this Ben City. It's where that fellow Park Justin runs a big ranch. Your business wouldn't be with him, would it?"

Ryker's gaze was reaching through the dust filmed window pane of the restaurant to the steadily increasing crowd in the street. Most everyone, it seemed, had waited until sundown and the evening's resultant coolness to do his shopping.

"Yeah, that's it," Clover said, getting no answer to his question. "Know all about this here Justin. He don't raise cattle to sell to the market, gets rid of them to other ranchers. That way he don't have to fool with drives and such. They say he does right well at it. You making a deal with him for some beef?"

"Could be," Ryker said, realizing he had

to make some sort of answer and get the subject dropped. "As soon you'd keep it quiet."

"Why? Nothing wrong with buying cattle from Park Justin is there?"

"No, but I've got me a sort of ticklish deal. Just don't want word getting out. Things going wrong could cause it all to blow up in my face, and leave me and my brother busted flat."

Nat Clover was silent for a time, then nodded sagely. "Sure, I savvy. You need any help? Be a pleasure to throw in with you, side you like I done in the old days. And I'm owing you a mighty big favor."

"No need. Obliged anyway, and you sure don't owe me anything," Jake replied, and paused, relieved to see the waitress coming through the kitchen's entrance with a platter of food in each hand. "Here's our grub. Sure ready for it."

They ate slowly, with relish, two trail-riding men who partook far too often of their own efforts over a campfire and knew how to genuinely appreciate the tasty handiwork of an expert in the kitchen.

Finished, they rose, paid their checks and, leaving a suitable tip for the girl with the semaphore hips, returned to the street.

Off to their right in front of the Empo-

74

rium a fight between two punchers was underway. Both were heaving back and forth, sweating, muttering curses, wrestling and flailing about with their fists while two dozen or more onlookers yelled advice and encouragement.

Standing on the boardwalk a short distance away and watching with little interest was a man wearing the star of the Texas side's town marshal. Farther down the row of buildings shots sounded in quick succession. The reports drew only passing notice from the crowd, none at all from the lawman.

"Figure to go back to the blackjack game?" Clover asked, probing at his broad teeth with a split match.

Two men with a young girl between them moved by. The girl was very drunk, head wobbling, eyes rolling wildly. One of her companions said something to her as they drew abreast. She laughed uncontrollably.

"Got me the feeling this is my night to buck the tiger," Nat continued, watching the three melt into the shifting crowd.

"Was having fair luck myself," Jake said. "Feel more like some poker, however."

"Always find a good game in the Lone Star."

Ryker nodded. "Won't hurt to have a look."

Pressing on, they reached the tall building, mounted the gallery and pushed through the scarred batwings into the saloon. Once there, they lowered their heads and bulled a course for the adjoining room, which was devoted entirely and exclusively to gambling.

"Hell of a lot of people around here, even for a Saturday night," Ryker said, wiping at the sweat on his face as he glanced around at the table. Practically every chair in the place was filled. The crowds around the faro and chuck-a-luck games were three deep.

"Bunch of drovers here, somebody said. Seven or eight different outfits, all closeby — all on their way home from Wichita and Dodge . . . You never did say for sure if you was dickering with Justin for beef."

"Brother's been talking to him," Jake said, still striving to avoid a direct answer. He knew Nat Clover probably as well as he did any man and figured him for one who could be trusted, but the less he or anyone else knew about the impending purchase, the better. Two thousand in cash was enough to tempt any man, even an honest one.

"Couple of chairs over there at that corner table? Want to set in?"

"I'm willing," Clover said, and led the way to the vacant seats.

An hour later, with Nat picked clean and wandering glumly about the room looking over shoulders, pausing now and then to talk with someone he knew, and Ryker down to his last double eagle, they abandoned the games.

"Figure to pull out early," Jake said as they wound their way toward the door. "Going to treat myself to a drink, then turn in. You stand a shot?"

"Sure could," Nat said, and then throwing a look over his shoulder at the men still at the table, added: "That goddam dealer — I ain't so sure but what he was reaching up his sleeve."

Ryker shook his head. "Wondered myself, considering the kind of cards he kept drawing. Watched close. Never saw anything that looked out of line. Expect he was just a better hand at cards than us."

They reached the connecting doorway that opened into the saloon, shoved up to the long counter. Leaning against it they ordered whiskey. Ryker paid, slid the change into his pocket. Taking up his glass, he wheeled lazily, hooked his elbows on

77

the rim of the mahogany bar and gazed out over the crowd in the stuffy, smoke-filled room.

"I'm still puzzling about that sharp," Nat Clover muttered at his shoulder. "Seems mighty funny to me, him getting such good cards."

Ryker, a frown on his sun and wind darkened face, was only half listening. Two men had ducked through the swinging doors just as he had come about. There was something familiar in the look of them, something that stirred a vague warning inside him.

He thought about it for several moments, brushed it from his mind. He guessed he was letting the worry of carrying two thousand dollars make him edgy. Taladega was a rough town but he had nothing to fear as long as he stayed clear of bawdy houses and the back alley saloons.

Tossing off the last of the liquor, he bucked his head at Clover. "I'm turning in. Expect you'll be staying over tomorrow."

The squat rider finished his drink. "Yeah, couple more days anyway. Got to see if I can raise me some cash now. Stripped clean. That goddam fancy dealing Cajun —"

"Short myself, but I've got a few extra

dollars you're welcome to."

Clover stared at Jake for a long breath, his features expressionless.

"Obliged," he said finally, "but I can get by. Can use my face for a little credit, enough to get on my feet. Appreciate your offering it to me."

"Welcome to it," Ryker said, and pushed away from the counter. He extended his hand. "If I don't see you later —"

Nat shrugged, ignored the gesture. "Might as well tramp on over to the Gold Dollar with you. I was doing pretty good there."

Again in the street, they angled through the throng and spinning dust for the opposite side. The crowd had increased, it seemed to Ryker, and he guessed the rumor Clover had heard concerning visiting drovers had been true.

They gained the sidewalk, stepped up onto it, began to thread a path for the hotel's entrance. Abreast the narrow passageway separating the hostelry from its adjacent neighbor on the north, motion in the darkness caught Jake's attention, brought him to a halt.

"Ryker!" a husky voice called from the darkness.

Instinctively Jake stepped to one side,

hand sweeping down for the pistol on his hip. Behind him he heard Nat Clover's voice.

"What the hell! Who's hiding in there?"

A gun blasted from the deep shadows, deafening in such narrow, confined quarters. Ryker fired at the flare of orange he saw dead ahead, heard the bullet that had been intended for him thud dully into the wall close by.

"Who is it?" Clover asked again, dropping to a crouch.

"Don't know," Jake rasped. "Somebody aiming to hold us up, I reckon. Keep down!"

In that next instant a pistol flashed once more in the blackness between the buildings. Jake Ryker staggered under a shocking blow to the head. Reflex triggered his own weapon clutched tightly in his hand, and then he fell forward into a pit of silent darkness.

IX

Vaguely, Ryker could hear shouts in the street: laughter, a rumbling of confusion as he slowly opened his eyes. Pain throbbed persistently in his head, and there was a paper dryness in his throat that made breathing difficult, recalling the time he found himself afoot in Arizona's Chiricahua desert country with no water.

"See you're still among the living . . ."

At the sound of the unfamiliar voice, the last of the cobwebby screen blocking his mind drifted away. He turned to a round-faced man with sweat shining on his cheeks, steel-rimmed spectacles circling his eyes, and a fringe of cottony hair ringing his head.

"I'm Doc Carmer. You got yourself a devil of a rap on the noggin."

Ryker looked down. He was lying on a couch in a room that smelled strongly of antiseptics. He stiffened as it all came to him in a quick, flooding rush. He was in a doctor's office. Somebody had lugged him there after the bushwhacking alongside the hotel . . . A bullet had struck him a glancing blow, laid him out cold.

Apprehension gripped him. His hands dropped to his waist, probed for the money belt. It was gone.

"Your gun?" Carmer asked. "Didn't figure you'd be needing it, lying there cold as a cucumber." He jerked his thumb toward a peg rack nailed to the papered wall. "It's hanging right there."

Jake struggled to a sitting position, swung his legs over the edge of the leather couch. The swirling nausea the effort created was as nothing compared to the sense of despair that filled him as he realized his loss. Hunched there on the smooth cowhide, he reached up, touched the side of his head, felt the bandage Carmer had wrapped about it.

"Best thing you can do is stay quiet."

"Can't," Jake Ryker said groggily. The two thousand dollars was gone. He groaned, thinking of what its loss meant to Tom and Callie — to him. He raised his gaze to the medical man.

"That all you took off me, my gun?"

Carmer nodded, frowned. "You missed something else?"

"Was wearing a money belt under my shirt."

82

"Never bothered to look there. Just got that belt and holster off you so's you could lie flat after the marshal and Ed Grimsby brought you in."

Jake's thoughts came to a halt. "What about the man with me — Nat Clover?"

"Clover?" Carmer shook his head. "Nobody with you, leastwise the marshal didn't say anything about it. They sure didn't carry anybody else in. Know who it was that jumped you?"

Clover had been crouched right behind him. It was strange that he, too, had not been hurt, or at least accompanied him to the doctor's office. Unless . . .

"No," he replied to Carmer's question, "but I'm getting a hunch. Which marshal was it?"

"Emerson. We're on the New Mexico side."

Jake Ryker got to his feet unsteadily. Carmer laid a hand on his shoulder. "Now, I'm not sure you're in any condition to —"

"Maybe not, but I've got to get to the bottom of this — quick," Ryker said, brushing the man's hand away and moving toward the peg rack. Reaching for his belt, he buckled it on, checked the pistol, and then dug into his pocket for the coins that should be there. He swore helplessly, with-

83

drew his hand. Whoever it was that had lain in wait for him in the dark, had stripped him.

Nat Clover. Ryker stood perfectly still as his thoughts swung again to the squat, scar-faced man. It wasn't possible! Yet Clover had questioned him considerably, had undoubtedly guessed he was carrying a fair amount of cash to make a cattle deal — and Clover hadn't been with him when the lawman and some passerby had carried him into Carmer's office . . . He thought he knew Nat Clover well, but he guessed a man could change, could fool his friends. And Nat was broke. A possible explanation came to him.

"You hear the marshal say whether there was anybody else there — dead?" he asked, hopefully.

"Was only you, unconscious from that bullet. I'd know. I'm the coroner here, too."

He reckoned that settled it. He had all the proof he needed; Clover had been with him, yet there was no sign of him when the shooting and robbery was all over. It was hard to believe, but a man was a fool to deny facts. Jake started to nod, thought better of it. He smiled wryly at Carmer.

"Got to owe you, Doc. They cleaned me out."

Carmer shrugged. "You're not the only member of the club. Two thirds of the county's on my cuff. There's always room for one more. Still don't think you ought to go galavanting around the shape you're in. Legs are liable to cave in under you if you get all worked up and overdo it. Show more sense to stay right there on that couch for the rest of the night."

"Expect you're right," Ryker admitted, "but it can't be done. Have to get back that money belt. More important than you might figure — than my head, for sure. First thing's to find out what happened to that partner of mine who was siding me."

"Emerson'll be the one to talk to. He got there just after the shooting started and found you."

Ryker drew on his hat carefully, cocking it to one side so as to not apply undue pressure on the throbbing wound above his temple.

"Obliged to you for the doctoring," he said, moving for the door. "You'll get your fee soon as I can put my hands on some money."

"The universal cry of the general public," Carmer murmured, smiling wea-

85

rily. "Take care — and good luck in finding your belt."

Ryker stepped out into the dust-filled night. The crowd had decreased but little and he guessed he'd been out for no more than an hour. Grim, still somewhat unsteady, he turned left, pointed for the lawman's office which, he recalled, was near the end of the street. Halfway, he met Emerson, heading back for the center of town.

"Marshal, like to ask you some questions. I'm —"

"Recognize you," the lawman said, coming to a stop. "You're the bird that got himself rapped good by a slug next to the hotel."

"That's me. Name's Ryker. Can you tell me what happened to my partner?"

"Partner? Didn't know you had one. Found only you, laying there bleeding like a gut shot dog."

That dull suspicion that had been building within Jake Ryker changed abruptly to absolute conviction. A coldness settled over him. Nat was one man he would have bet on. Features stiff, he faced the lawman again.

"You the first one to find me?"

"Was. Had been standing a few doors

86

down. Heard the shooting."

"And by the time you got there whoever it was that shot me was gone — along with my partner?"

"Reckon so. I got there fairly fast, but there was a lot of folks milling about, and I wasn't so sure where the shots come from. Whoever they were, they'd gone."

"They? Something make you figure there was more than one?"

"No way of telling. Just a way of saying it. Maybe come daylight we might puzzle it out, but I misdoubt it. Lots of trash and such blowed in there. Wouldn't be no tracks."

Emerson paused, watched a half a dozen belted and spurred punchers weave in from the opposite side of the street, slant for one of the lesser saloons. He brought his small, dark eyes back to Jake.

"Hell, getting robbed ain't nothing special around here. Comes along pretty often, man getting hisself knocked flat on his ass and his money took. You ought to figure yourself lucky you ain't dead. There's plenty of them end up that way."

"Not just a matter of a few dollars. I was wearing a money belt, aimed to buy some cattle. Was quite a bit of cash in it."

Emerson pursed his lips, fingered his

mustache. "Didn't know about that." He frowned. "Can tell you this much, I was the first man on the spot, like I already said. Nobody'd touched you yet. I looked to see if you was dead or alive. You was breathing so I hollered at Ed Grimsby. He was standing at the end of the passageway holding folks back. Told him to give me a hand. You ask Doc Carmer about the belt?"

"Said the only thing he took off me was my gun."

"That'll be the truth. Doc ain't the lying kind. And I sure'n hell never glommed onto it. This partner of yours you mentioned — you real sure about him? Seems kind of funny, him disappearing the way he has."

"It's got me to wondering," Jake replied.

"You see him talking to anybody before you two come walking by that alley?"

Ryker's thoughts cut back to the Lone Star. Nat had wandered about the room, had spoken to several men he evidently knew.

"Remember now that he did. Over in the Lone Star's gambling parlor. He'd gone broke, was just stalling around waiting for me."

Emerson nodded sagely. "Thing's starting to make sense. Way I see it, he ought've been there beside you, either hurt or dead, or else still shooting at whoever it was that laid for you — but there wasn't no sign of him. That how you see it?"

Ryker, features expressionless, only nodded. He stared off into the crowded, noisy street with its restless throng and hovering clouds of dust. "How long ago did this happen? Was out so I've got no idea of time."

"Been a couple hours, more or less. Mostly less, I'd say. You want to give me a description of that partner of yours? Maybe I can spot him?"

"He'd be long gone by now," Ryker said heavily. "Obliged to you just the same." He was yet finding it hard to believe that Nat Clover would turn on him, sell him out, but the evidence, however circumstantial, was undeniable. "I'll do my own looking — and settling up."

Wheeling, he started through the crowd for the Gold Dollar. Halfway there a thought came to him, and circling the hotel, he crossed to the stable in the rear. The hostler came forward to meet him at once, one cheek bulging with tobacco.

"You know Nat Clover?" Jake said without ceremony.

The old man rubbed at the back of his neck. "Clover?" he repeated. "Seems I ought . . . What's he look like?"

"Little on the short side. Heavy. Got a scar on his face."

"Him — oh sure! Rides a spotted Indian pony."

"That's the man. He been here tonight?"

"You bet he was. Come in a couple hours back. Was in a powerful hurry. Had me saddle his horse, then took off like the heel flies was after him."

A tautness filled Jake Ryker. "Anybody with him?"

The old man spat a brown stream at the base of the livery stable wall. "Nope. All by hisself."

Ryker studied the oldster's lined features. "You see which way he went?"

"Sure did. Took the Trail."

The Trail. The Taladega Trail: a road that ran straight south to Mexico. Jake Ryker swore silently. It had been all set up; Nat would meet the man or men who'd been in on the holdup with him at the edge of town after it was all over. Then, all would line out fast for the border.

"Be needing my horse," he said abruptly. "In a hurry myself — it's the chestnut with the diamond brand on his hip."

"Know which one. Was me that rubbed him down, done the feeding —"

"Be back for him soon's I get my saddlebags."

"Aiming to pull out for good?"

Half turned away, Ryker gave that thought. He had no cash with which to pay off, and if the hostler and the hotel clerk believed him to be leaving, he could run into delay and difficulties.

"Just aiming to catch up with my fri— with Clover," he said and hurried on.

There was no one at the hotel's desk when he entered the lobby. Climbing the stairs, he picked up his bags, made sure all his belongings were inside, and returned to the lower floor. The clerk was still nowhere to be seen. Taking up the pencil he found lying beside the register, he located a scrap of paper and wrote: *Will settle later. J. Ryker.*, and placed it between the pages of the book where it would be found.

That done, he returned to the stable. The hostler had the gelding ready and Ryker swung immediately to the saddle. Wheeling the big horse about, he hesitated, gazed down at the elderly man.

"You're dead sure Clover took the Trail south?"

"Sure as I'm standing here. Was right

91

here in the yard and seen him do it."

"Was dark. He might've turned west."

"Dang it, he didn't! Don't take much light to see a man on a spotted horse riding straight away and keeping on going straight! There's a bright moon out there once a man gets out of all this dust."

"For a fact," Jake said. "Hadn't noticed," and rode off the hard pack.

The moon should prove to be a big help.

X

The cool night air served as a tonic and stimulant. Riding across the flat on a course paralleling the road, the dull ache in Ryker's head became less noticeable and his mind clearer. The hostler had been right; away from the settlement and its scuffling, restless occupants, the moon was strong and a silver radiance flooded the country, turned it almost to daylight.

He twisted about, looked back to Taladega. A pale glare hung over the town like a canopy. From the distance it lent a beautiful effect, but he realized it was no more than heavy layers of suspended dust against which lamps threw their yellow glow.

Morose, he turned his attention to the country stretched before him. He was purposely avoiding the road, not wanting to betray his presence by the hoof beats of the chestnut on its hard-baked surface. It was slower going in the loose sand but he felt the time lost was more than offset by the silence he could thus preserve.

There was still a nagging reluctance within him to believe Nat Clover had been a part of the robbery. But the indications were there, and it all boiled down to a single point; only Nat had any idea that he was carrying a large sum of money on his person — and even that had been a logical assumption on the scar-faced man's part.

Nat, by sheer coincidence, had known of Park Justin, had jumped to the correct conclusion that a cattle deal was in the making; and since Justin dealt on a strictly cash basis, it necessarily followed that anyone buying a herd from him would be carrying money.

Thus, who else could it have been but Nat? If a man needed further proof he had but to consider Clover's unexplained disappearance in the passageway; and then his hasty departure from the settlement. There could be no question.

A gust of anger whipped through Jake Ryker. He would've been a hell of a lot better off if he'd let Ford and the rest of the Circle R cowhands string Clover up to that cottonwood! He'd still have Tom's two thousand dollars buckled around his belly and not be riding off into the night on what was probably a hopeless attempt to recover it.

Hopeless . . . Hell, he couldn't look at it that way! He had to get that money back somehow. Otherwise, Tom and Callie and the Circle R were busted flat — and he would have proved just what they always thought of him, that he was a shiftless, worthless saddle bum, completely irresponsible and basically dishonest.

That's what Callie would certainly think. She'd make up her mind about him quick, and then with that acid-tipped tongue of hers, declare that he'd probably cached the money somewhere where he'd later recover it, while he came up with a cock-and-bull yarn about getting robbed — right in the middle of a town! That's what Callie Ryker would want to believe, and being who she was, that's what she actually would believe.

Well, she was going to be disappointed. She'd not get the chance to think that of him. He'd find Nat Clover and the man or men who were mixed up in the ambush with him, and get back the money if he had to chase them clear across Mexico.

But he'd have to do it fast. And he realized he was lucky he was able to do anything about it at all. He was lucky to be alive when you came right down to it. That bullet had come within a fraction of putting him in the graveyard.

Staring off across the moonlit country, all soft and gentle looking under the pale shine, he gingerly probed the portion of his head under Carmer's bandage. There was a rawness to it. He swore angrily as he flinched. That damned Clover, if he —

Something — motion — off to the left of the trail a short distance down the way brought him up sharply. Reining in the chestnut, he raised himself in the stirrups and endeavored to make out what it was that had alerted his senses. An animal of some kind; a wolf or a coyote, maybe. Seemed larger, however. Could be a stray from some nearby herd of cattle.

He wouldn't accept any of those explanations for one reason — he was unsure. Roweling the gelding lightly, he sent him forward at a slow walk. Pistol in hand, he kept his eyes riveted to the dim, dark shape off to the side.

It was a horse. Jake, puzzled by the appearance of the animal, evidently abandoned, so far from the settlement, pressed on quietly. Abruptly he pulled the chestnut to a halt again. It was Nat Clover's spotted pony.

Directly opposite the horse Ryker dismounted. Tying the chestnut to a clump of chamiso, he moved toward the road carefully, not sure of what it all meant, it could be a trap of some sort.

He reached the shoulder of the road, hunched in behind a thick stand of brush. The pinto was ten yards away. Head down, reins dragging, the horse still carried its gear. There was no sign of Clover.

Suspicion plucking at him, Jake dropped back, continued along the road to a point where, hidden from the pinto, he crossed over. Then, doubling back up the opposite shoulder he approached the pony from its off side.

He saw Nat's body. The scar-faced man lay in a shallow ravine a few steps from his horse. When he had fallen from the saddle, the leathers had dropped also, and the well-trained animal, ground-reined, had come to an immediate halt.

What the hell was going on?

Ryker, squatted on his heels, worked at the problem. Had Clover's friends turned on him, deciding not to share the contents of the belt? The question disturbed Jake but he did not move in for a closer look and possible explanation just yet; it could be a ruse, a trap. Thus, he continued to watch and wait in the shadowy brush, listening, testing the breeze for the smell of tobacco smoke or other distinctive odors that would indicate other men lurking nearby.

Nothing. Finally convinced there was no one around, Ryker moved out of hiding and, still cautious and quiet in his actions, stepped to where Clover lay.

Nat had been taken from behind. There were two bullet wounds in his back. Jake rolled the man over, stared at the slack features, noting the dark bruise over the right eye. Nat had never known what hit him, he guessed; the bullets had been fired from either side and at close range with unavoidable accuracy; his own forty-five was still in its holster.

Jake Ryker felt no stir of pity for the scar-faced man. He'd chosen to run with wolves, therefore he had to expect the treatment of wolves. Crossing to the pinto, he pulled off the saddle and bridle, turned the animal loose. He would be better off shifting for himself unencumbered by tack.

Dropping then to his knees beside the worn hull, Jake examined the contents of the saddlebags. Finding nothing of interest to him, he returned to Clover's body, went through the dead man's pockets. He failed to turn up anything that would be of help there either.

Rising, Ryker returned to the waiting

chestnut and mounted. One thing certain — he was on the right trail. Clover and the others had headed south out of Taladega, unquestionably making for the border. Thinking about it, he reckoned he'd run into a bit of good luck; Nat's partners, now rid of him, could be just taking it easy. They believed him dead back in the settlement, and with Clover now also permanently out of the picture, they would feel the need to quickly vanish had been removed.

Clucking the gelding into motion, Ryker pushed on, still avoiding the hard surface of the Trail, having his thoughts and wondering about Nat Clover, while his eyes searched ahead continually for indications of riders.

Nat's killing disturbed him. There was no reason for it other than the fact that his partners did not wish to share the money in the belt with him. But the fact that he, and not someone else, was the leader, the instigator of the holdup would tend to make that reasoning illogical. Nat would have picked men he could control.

Too, Clover had departed the Gold Dollar's stable alone and in a big hurry. Why hadn't they all ridden out together? Such would be more reasonable and understandable. Clover and those with him, slipping out of the passageway before anyone else had time to appear and leaving the town as a single party made sense. Nat's departure some time later did not.

The matter became more confusing as Jake rolled it about in his mind. There were just too many things that didn't jibe, too many parts in the puzzle that didn't fit.

Time wore on and the long, lonely miles of a hushed, barren land, turned eerily beautiful by the moon and stars, moved endlessly by. The pain in his head began to increase, whetted no doubt by the jogging of the chestnut, the sense of loss and frustration that possessed him, and the strain of pushing a body that needed rest and care.

It would be hard to trace the money if he lost the riders, he realized, as he had no idea of who they were or what they looked like — assuming there was more than one, which he was now inclined to believe; the two holes in Clover's back made by bullets coming from different angles tended to prove that.

While Nat was a member of the party and with the others, he would have had no difficulty in tracking them down, since it was possible to recognize and if necessary describe Nat. But that was out now, and facing that, he admitted how difficult his job would be unless he could overtake the outlaws before they could give him the slip.

Ryker's jaw came to a grim set. He couldn't, wouldn't let that happen. He had to catch up with them before they shook him off the trail — or the money would be lost forever. Searching for men he did not know and had no idea of their appearances or names would be a hopeless task no matter how determined he might be.

All such dark thoughts and considerations washed suddenly from his mind. On the brow of a hill he pulled the chestnut to a quick stop. Satisfaction stirred through him, filled him with a harsh grimness and relief.

Not a hundred yards away a small campfire flared in the shadow of a butte. Two men were hunched nearby. They were sorting something on the ground before them.

XI

Jake Ryker dropped softly to the ground. Again tethering the chestnut, he went to all fours, and keeping in a shallow, brush-lined wash, crept in close to the two men. Their words reached him before he was near enough to see them clearly.

"Was pure damn luck us nailing that jasper that was following us . . ."

Ryker, flat on the cool ground, stiffened. The voice had a familiar tone. He racked his memory for some clue, some recollection of the past; it came to him suddenly. It was Lenny Gault.

"Well, he sure won't be following nobody else! You can bet your aces on that."

Chuck Virden had made the answer — and they were speaking of Nat Clover! A stab of conscience caused Jake Ryker to stir. It hadn't been the way he'd figured at all; Nat had evidently been chasing the pair hoping to recover the money belt for him. The scar-faced rider had not double-crossed him, had instead been trying to

102

help . . . That bruise on his head — that probably explained why he had been slow in leaving the settlement in pursuit; he had been injured, too.

Anger shook Jake Ryker as it all became clearer to him. Gault and Virden had then heard Clover coming, had pulled off the road to hide. When Nat passed they closed in from either side, shot him in the back. Ryker's fingers moved to the butt of his pistol in a spasm of anger. Then, jaw clamped tight, he wormed his way in to where he could see the hunched men.

They were counting the money taken from the belt, were dividing it into equal piles. Gault, handling the worn bills, laughed.

"Know what's funny about this? Us a squaring up with that sonofabitching Ryker for Ed and Tolly and getting paid for it!"

Chuck grinned, nodded. "Had him fooled for sure. Expect he figured them sod-busters back in Lordsburg still had us cornered."

They'd been on his trail all the way, Jake realized, had probably been a half a day behind him. He may have shaken them while he was at the Circle R, but if so it had been only briefly, for they were in

Taladega while he was there. He knew now that these were the two men he'd caught a glimpse of as they ducked through the doorway at the Lone Star. From there they had gone to the alleyway beside the hotel and lain in wait for him.

"Mighty glad you spotted that belt when you was going through his pockets. Undertaker'd a got it for sure."

"Sort of makes up for us finding nothing on that bird siding him."

"Made up!" Virden laughed again. "I'd say it more'n made up."

He had the complete picture now. The pair had followed him to Taladega, watching for a chance to avenge the deaths of Ed Virden and the man they'd called Tolly. Their moment had come when Nat and he were passing the narrow alleyway next to the Gold Dollar. They had thought him dead, probably had figured Nat Clover was also. Then they had rifled their pockets. Finding the money belt had been an accident.

"This is sure going to set us up good," Lenny Gault said, wetting a thumb and resuming the apportioning. "Why, down in Mexi—"

"It's going to hang both of you

bastards!" Jake Ryker snarled, and rose to his full height from the shadows.

A startled oath burst from Gault's lips. Virden froze momentarily, then made a desperate stab for the pistol on his hip. In that same fraction of time Gault lunged, scooped up a double handful of fire and ashes, flung them straight at Ryker's face.

Jake instinctively threw up an arm to protect his eyes, fired point-blank at Chuck Virden. The outlaw jolted, went over backward as the heavy bullet smashed into him.

Feeling the burn of the live coals in several places, choking on the powdery ash, Ryker rocked to one side, dropped to his knees as he sought to locate Lenny Gault. An instant later Ryker saw him. Gault was still near the scattered fire frantically trying to collect the money now strewn before him and draw his weapon at the same time. Jake threw a bullet into the ground in front of the outlaw. His eyes still smarted and stung and he was having trouble seeing clearly.

But the slug drove Gault back. He dropped the bills he'd gathered, managed to trigger off a shot. Jake snapped a reply at the dim, weaving shape, missed. An instant later Gault spun, flung himself back into the deep shadows of the brush a stride behind him. Jake again knuckling his eyes, fired once more, his only target a vague, fleeting shape. Gault cursed in the dark as luck rode the bullet, found its mark.

Ryker, vision now improving, avoided the flare of the dying fire, crossed to his left and raced forward for another shot. The sudden, hard tattoo of a horse moving away fast reached him. He pulled up short, anger and tension beating at him furiously.

"Run for it you sonofabitch!" he shouted in an exasperated voice. "But you'll not get away from me!"

Spinning, he ran back to the fire. Casting only a side glance at Chuck Virden's still figure, he slid his pistol into its holster, and dropping to a crouch, gathered in the bills and gold pieces, crammed them back into the money belt. Then, rising, he started for the chestnut at a hard run, taking time only to cram the money belt inside his shirt. Later he'd buckle it on properly; at the moment catching Gault, making him pay for Nat Clover's death was more important.

Reaching the gelding, he yanked the leathers free and vaulted onto the saddle. Roweling the big chestnut savagely, he sent him plunging ahead into the night. Gault

106

was hit; he knew that, but just how bad he did not know. The outlaw had chosen to run, however, and not shoot it out. Such made it appear he was in a bad way.

He wasn't in too good a condition himself, he thought as the gelding pounded on through the moonlight-filled night. Dizziness was bothering him again. He supposed it was the result of exertion and strain. Carmer had warned him not to overdo anything.

The burns he'd sustained were minor: a place here and there on his forearms and neck where live coals and sparks had settled when Gault tossed the fire at him. It was the ash powder that had reached his eyes that troubled him most. But they would clear up in time.

Leaning forward, he brushed at them, endeavoring to wipe away the mistiness that persisted in gathering, and peered ahead. He wasn't sure, but he thought he could make out the dim outline of a rider. Urging the chestnut to faster speed, he drew his pistol, tossed away the spent cartridges, thumbed in fresh loads.

He saw Gault a few minutes later. The outlaw, a blurred shape, was bent low over his saddle. His horse was running erratically, almost wildly, either tiring or endeavoring to respond to heavy, faltering hands.

Once more Ryker called on the chestnut for speed. The big red eased ahead, began to close the gap that separated him from the animal Gault rode. Jake saw Gault straighten partly, half turn, throw a glance over his shoulder. Immediately the outlaw swerved his mount off the road, struck out across open country.

Jake veered the gelding from the hard-packed surface of the trail, and followed closely. Gault's horse was in trouble, seemed to be breaking under the hard drive. All the signs were there. The chestnut needed only to keep pressing.

Suddenly Lenny Gault's mount went down. The outlaw hit hard in a flurry of dust and sand, came unsteadily to his feet. Jake, caught by the suddenness of it all, swerved the gelding to one side. He saw the bright orange flash of the pistol in Gault's hand, felt the searing burn of a bullet cutting across the upper part of his arm.

Deadly cool, he fired at the dim, weaving shape of the outlaw, fired again. Gault staggered, went to his knees, and then fell forward.

Jake brought the plunging chestnut to a stop, a strange wheeling sensation spinning through his brain. Motionless on the saddle of the heaving horse, one hand still clutching his weapon, the other the leather-covered horn, he stared at the outlaw through misty eyes. After a bit the whirling ceased and his vision cleared somewhat. He urged the chestnut in nearer to the man, halted. There was no need to dismount and examine Lenny Gault, even if he could muster the strength and the will. The outlaw was dead.

Reaching deep for a breath, he shook himself. It was over with. He had avenged Nat Clover, had recovered the money belt with its cash. He became aware then of the stinging on his arm, of a warm stickiness along his elbow. Unaccountably, temper flared through him.

"Dammit to hell!" he shouted into the night as frustration and anger swept him. What kind of luck was plaguing him? Why was everything going wrong? He'd started out on a simple mission of buying a herd of cattle; he'd been bushwhacked, nearly killed, shot, half blinded, and lost a good friend and in the process, forced to gun down two men . . . What the hell would happen next?

One thing was for damn sure! Tom and Callie could have the ranch. Their way of life! He'd stick to his, and he'd pick it up just as soon as he could get the herd back to the Circle R and hire on a man to run things. He'd had enough.

Muttering, he looked down at his arm. The wound was a raw, red splotch in the fleshy part above the elbow. Gault's bullet had carved a deep groove in its burning passage. It was bleeding freely. Still caught up in a strange light-headedness, Ryker dug out his handkerchief, wrapped it about the wound, and with teeth and fingers managed to pull the corners into a fairly tight knot. The effort sent his brain to spinning more furiously, and he settled back, waited for it to subside, then urged the gelding into forward motion. Best he go back to Taladega . . . see Doc Carmer again . . . get fixed up. . . .

. . . The chestnut was not moving. Jake Ryker became aware of that, aware also that a broad sheet of pearl filled the sky to the east and that sunrise was not far off. He looked about, dazed.

Nothing appeared familiar. The gelding must have wandered for hours on its own. Jake raised a hand, brushed back his hat. A short distance ahead he saw a narrow, sandy wash beyond which a slight grade led to a stand of trees. The faint sparkle of a stream cut across the slope at the edge of the grove. That's what he needed, what would help — water. He'd get down, give his head a good, cool soaking. It should rid him of the dizziness.

The chestnut, smelling the stream, moved out eagerly without being urged by the spurs. He crossed the arroyo, ascended the slope and pointed for the trees. At once two riders broke out of the deep shadows, fanned out, barred his way. Ryker hauled back on the gelding's reins, brought him to a stop.

"Now, what the hell do you want?" he demanded as a fresh surge of frustration and anger rolled through him.

XII

Mind clearing fast, Ryker's hand drifted to the butt of his pistol. Eyes narrowed, he took in the pair: a thin-faced dark man and a husky, hard-jawed blond. A cold resoluteness filled Jake; nobody was going to get the money belt again — not without one hell of a fight. He put his question to them again.

"What's on your mind?"

"Reckon the first thing," a voice from behind him drawled, "will be for you to take your paw off that shooting iron unless you want me to blow it off."

Ryker stiffened, allowed his fingers to slide away. He cast a look over his shoulder. A third man had come from the brush, a small, wiry rider who looked as if he might be part Mexican or perhaps Indian. He was holding a cocked rifle in his hands. Ryker cursed himself for his carelessness. He knew better than to leave himself wide open like that, but somehow he wasn't thinking as straight as he should.

The narrow-faced one grinned crookedly, bobbed his head. "That's better."

112

"All right, it's better!" Ryker snapped. "What's this all about?"

Again the man's mouth split into a smile. "Just you listen to him, boys! It's like maybe he don't know."

The speaker moved around to join the others, directing his horse with pressure from his knees while he kept the long gun leveled at Jake. The blond shoved his hat to the back of his head, shrugged.

"He ain't that dumb."

"Reckon I am," Ryker said blandly, "leastwise to what you're yapping about." His head was functioning normally now, and he was conscious of only a dull ache. "Happens I'm riding across country. That a crime or something in this part of Texas?"

"All depends," the narrow-faced man said. "Pull his fangs, Charlie."

The blond moved in behind Jake, halted close by. Reaching forward, he lifted Ryker's weapon from its holster, pulled away, frowning.

"He's been in some kind of a ruckus, Bud. Got wrappings on his head and his arm's been bleeding."

"I sure am sorry," the rider replied dryly. "Get at it, Frank. Shake out that there rope of your'n."

113

Frank unhooked his riata from the saddle horn. Charlie frowned again, rubbed at his ear. "You ain't aiming to string him up, are you?"

"Sure what we ought to do!" Bud said. "Teague's been told to keep off Medford range, and it'd be smart to put some teeth in the old man's warnings, let that Rocking T bunch know we're plumb tired of being hoorawed and kicked around."

Ryker, motionless on the saddle, mouth set to a thin line, listened in silence. This was no holdup. He'd blundered, instead, into some sort of range trouble. When the man called Bud had finished, he shook his head.

"You've got me wrong, friend. I don't know anybody named Teague or Medford, and I've never heard of the Rocking T."

"Yeah, I'll bet," Bud said scornfully. "How about that loop, Frank?"

"It's the truth," Ryker insisted. "I'm from over New Mexico way, the Circle R ranch. Brother's name is Tom Ryker. Could be you've heard of him?"

"Nope, never heard of him, same as you ain't never heard of nobody I've mentioned. What's more I don't believe a goddam word you've spoke!"

Jake's shoulders came back slowly.

114

Somewhere in the fields below the trees a meadowlark was pealing out its song.

"Don't like being called a liar," Ryker said quietly.

Bud laughed. "You ain't going to like a lot of things that'll be happening to you in a couple of minutes! We're owing you Rocking T yahoos a plenty, and now you're going to get a little payment on account. See what it's like to be on the getting end of all this hoorawing you been dishing out."

"I'll tell you again, I've got nothing to do with the Rocking T outfit —"

"Drop that rope around him, Frank."

The half-breed shaped a loop. Charlie held up a hand, stayed the rider. "Maybe we'd best take him to see Medford first, let him decide."

"Hell, the old man's run plumb out of guts. He'd just turn him loose."

"Could be that's what we ought to do, too. Maybe he ain't one of Teague's crew. Sure ain't never seen him around here before."

"That ain't no surprise. Cowhands come and go real regular like on the Rocking T."

"Sure, but I still figure we —"

"Now, mister," Bud shouted, suddenly out of patience, "if you want to trot over

115

and tell the old man what we're doing, you go right ahead. Me and Frank's got a better idea. Come on — get that lasso around him!"

Frank swung in quickly, dropped a loop around Ryker's middle, jerked it tight before Jake could throw it off.

"We dragging him — that what you're planning?" Frank asked, throwing his weight against the line to keep it taut.

Bud bobbed his head. "Just what I got in mind. Maybe if we scatter a little Rocking T hide across Medford range, Teague's bunch won't be so anxious to jump any of us next time we meet up."

Ryker's fingers wrapped about the riata encircling his waist, loosened its choking grasp. Instantly Frank spurred away. Jake came off the saddle with a jerk. He struck the ground on his right shoulder, groaned at the solid impact. His senses reeled briefly as pain shot through him, but taking a tight grip on himself, he managed to recover balance and come upright.

Legs spraddled, eyes blazing, he faced the three riders. "This'll be something you'll regret —"

"Sure we will," Bud cut in with a laugh. "But I reckon it won't be half as much as you'll be doing. We're up to our ears with

116

you Rocking T waddies running around taking potshots at us, acting like you owned the whole goddam country. I'm aiming to give you a swallow of your own medicine."

Ryker's anger settled into a cold stream. He wasn't being robbed of the cash he carried, and that was one thing he could be thankful for; but he was not looking forward to being dragged across the flats as an object lesson to others he had no knowledge of or connection with.

"Telling you again — you're making a mistake. I don't work for this Teague you keep talking about. Better play it smart, take me to Medford, if he's your boss, like Charlie there says before it's too late."

"Too late for what?" Bud demanded, leaning forward. A sly grin pulled down the corners of his mouth.

Ryker could feel the warm stickiness above his elbow again. The fall from the saddle had started the wound in his arm to bleeding again.

"You and me will have some settling up to do when this is over. I won't be letting it pass."

"Doubt if you'll be in shape to do much of anything, 'cepting patch your hide. Get going, Frank!"

117

The lean cowhand looped the rope around his forearm, dug spurs into the buckskin he was riding. The horse leaped away and Bud and the blond Charlie swung in beside him, both yelling.

Desperate, Jake Ryker threw himself to the nearest tree, placed it between himself and the departing riders. The rope went taut against the cottonwood's unbending trunk. Bracing himself with stiffened knees and the heels of his boots digging into the soil, Ryker laid his weight against the tough strands of the lariat.

The rope snapped to a rigid line. Frank, having neglected to anchor his end to the saddle but winding it around his arm instead, catapulted backward off the buckskin, slammed hard to the ground.

Pain roaring through him, breathless from the shock and wrench of the rope, its sharp jerk only partly absorbed by the tree, Ryker lunged forward, fell upon the stunned rider. His hand darted out and closed upon the pistol in its holster.

Bud and Charlie, taken by surprise at the swift change, hauled up short. The narrow-faced rider swore loudly as anger swept him.

"You damned fool!" he roared at Frank. "Ain't you got sense enough to throw a dally around your horn instead of trying to hold a rope with your hand?"

"Never mind him," Ryker said coldly. "Just keep your hands where I can see them." He shifted his attention to Charlie. "You — climb down, walk over here. Try dropping your arms and you're dead."

The blond came off his horse hurriedly, crossed to where Jake stood.

"Back up to me."

Charlie complied obediently. Ryker recovered his own pistol from the puncher's waistband, relieved the man of his weapon.

"Now, you," he called then to Bud.

Muttering under his breath, the rider dismounted. Jake put him through the same procedure. Afterward he pointed at Frank, now stirring feebly. "Load him on his horse."

Bud and Charlie wrestled the man to his feet, got him onto the buckskin, and turned. The blond's eyes were wary.

"What's next? You taking us to Teague's so's your bunch can work us over good?"

"No, you're taking me to this Medford you keep talking about," Ryker answered, backing slowly to the chestnut. He had the inclination to step up to Bud, clout him soundly alongside the head as an object lesson, but his own wounds were throbbing. It could wait.

Charlie frowned. "Medford?"

Keeping his gun on the three men, Jake swung up to the saddle, eased himself into the tree.

"Mount up and head out. I'll be three jumps behind you all the time with my iron pointing at your backbones. And the way I'm feeling right now, you'd best not worry me."

"But — Medford —"

"Move!" Ryker snapped impatiently, and drew back the hammer of his forty-five.

XIII

They rode due south for a time, finally broke over a low ridge, came out at once into a much greener country where the grass grew thick and more trees were in evidence. For a while they followed out a broad swale, and then once again topped a hogback, where they looked down upon a large lake shimmering like blue-tinted crystal in the bright sunlight.

Despite the ache in his head, the throbbing soreness of his arm, Jake Ryker stirred in admiration. Medford, whoever he was, had a fine range. He'd seen little as good anywhere, in fact. He began to notice cattle, many small herds of four or five hundred animals, an occasional group of less, all drifting leisurely along or else grazing on the lush forage.

Questions came to Jake Ryker's mind that he would like to ask of the men riding sullenly in front of him, but he held his tongue. He was in no mood for friendly conversation, and considering that he had turned the trick on them and was driving them home under the sights of his pistol, he doubted very much they would be in a talkative frame of mind either.

But whatever the nature of the trouble Medford was having with the man the punchers called Teague, the rancher certainly had every reason to fight for his land. He could only wish the Circle R was as fine.

Beyond the swale where the lake lay, they came out onto a broad plain that seemed to have neither high nor low areas. Grass was again plentiful, and the purple heads of the slender stalks nodded and shifted in the light breeze constantly, changing the mesa into a restless ocean. Many trees were to be seen, and well off to their right Jake caught sight of a tall line of darker green growth in front of which were several structures. That would be Medford's ranch.

He sighed deeply, brushed at the sweat on his face. It would be a relief to climb off the gelding, get some medical attention for his irritating if not serious wounds, and grab a little food and rest; too, it would be good to shed himself of Bud and his two companions.

They rode into the deserted yard, pulled up to a hitchrack placed beneath a spreading hackberry near the end of the house. It was a place dedicated strictly to business, Jake noted, glancing around. Medford had no womenfolk on the premises, he guessed. There were no frills, no light touches to break the monotonous scene. Everything was of definite need and of practical use.

"Where'll Medford be?" he asked, swinging his attention to the three punchers, halted and still in the saddle, awaiting his direction.

"Who the hell knows?" Bud demanded courtly. "Might try yelling."

"Can do better than that," Ryker said curtly, and pointing his pistol skyward, pressed off a shot.

At the blast of the weapon, the riders jumped. A voice sang out from inside the barn, and a dog came rushing up from behind the corrals barking furiously. The kitchen shack's screen door flung open, banged against the wall of the clapboard building.

"That him?" Ryker asked, eyeing the elderly man who had appeared.

"Naw, he's the cook," Charlie answered. "That there's the boss coming up from the barn."

Jake turned about. "Sit easy," he said

quietly as Frank made a move to leave the saddle. "Want the lot of you where I can watch you."

Bud swore. "Hell, we ain't figuring to run."

"You sure as hell better not try," Ryker said mildly. "But with no more brains than you've showed, I'm not taking any chances."

Medford was a loose-jointed, thin man of sixty or so with almost no hair. He moved across the yard at a shambling gait, head pitched forward, small dark eyes sparking hotly. He halted at the end of the rack, took in his three hired hands along with Ryker and his drawn pistol all in one swift glance.

"What the devil's going on here?"

"Caught him trespassing," Bud began hurriedly, and then halted as a half-smile broke the rancher's lips.

"You caught him? Appears to me it's the other way around." He faced Ryker. "Who're you, mister?"

"We figured him for one of Teague's bunch." Charlie explained.

Jake shrugged. "Happens I'm not. Name's Jake Ryker. I'm from New Mexico. Brother and me have got a spread on the Pecos — the Circle R."

"He was on your range," Bud insisted doggedly, "and he sure looks like one of them Rocking T gunnies."

Jake shrugged. "Your hired hands are plenty hard to convince. Truth is, I've never heard of Teague — or of you either until I run into these three."

Medford plucked at his stringy mustache, eyes touching the bandage on Ryker's head, the bloodstained handkerchief wrapped about his arm.

"I'll be begging your pardon for them, Mr. Ryker. They was just looking out for me — and we're all a mite jumpy. Could say they was just doing what they figured was needful."

"Dragging a man across the flats — that's needful? I come close to parting with some hide."

"Glad you stopped it — and it looks like Frank there got the worst of whatever they started. It all right if they head over to the bunkhouse where he can get fixed up?"

Jake Ryker's shoulders stirred indifferently. He pulled the pistols he'd collected from the three punchers from his saddlebags, handed them over.

"Was aiming to have a few words with Bud, but I reckon I can forget it."

"Be obliged if you will. Like I said, they

125

was only thinking of me. Expect you'd better come on into the house. Seems you could use a little fixing yourself. They do that?"

Ryker shook his head, came off the chestnut. "Some trouble I had back on the Trail." He paused there, his thoughts going to Nat Clover, to Gault and Chuck Virden. He wished there had been something he could do about their bodies. Leaving them there for the vultures and the coyotes was wrong, but he'd had no choice.

Maybe he could do something about further trouble, however; he'd had his fill of that. Turning to Medford, he said: "One thing I'd like to mention while it's in my mind. I'm heading east for the Brazos country, Park Justin's place. Looks like I'll be on your range for a spell. If all of your hands are as touchy as these birds, I'd like a letter or something from you telling them I'm not against you."

Medford smiled faintly, nodded to Bud and the others who immediately pulled away from the rack and angled across the yard for the long, low-roofed building that evidently was the crew's quarters.

"Can sure fix that," the rancher said, leading the way toward the main house. "And you'll need it, I can tell you that. It's like a war was going on around here. How about a cup of coffee? Cook'll have some hotted up on the stove."

"Would taste mighty good," Ryker said, sinking into one of the several chairs scattered about on the porch. Out of the saddle, and with the lessening of tension, he was feeling somewhat better. Laying his hat aside, he watched Medford limp to the edge of the gallery, look toward the kitchen.

"Angus! Bring some coffee! Two cups," he yelled. Wheeling, he returned to where Jake was seated, drew back a chair for himself.

"What's all the fireworks about?" Ryker asked, when the older man was settled.

At that moment, Angus, the man Jake had seen earlier in the doorway of the cookshack, came into the open. He crossed the yard to the porch, carrying the cups and a gray enamel pot. Setting them all on the table, he stared curiously at Ryker for a moment, then retraced his steps to his kitchen.

"Way those hands of yours talked, this Teague must be a real hell-raiser."

"Ain't no guessing about that," Medford said wearily, filling the cups with steaming, black liquid. Putting the pot to one side, he sank back glumly, small, dark eyes on the floor.

"Teague's out to ruin me, bust me flat," he said. "And the way it's shaping up, he's going to do it."

Ryker brushed sweat from his face and neck. "Range war?" he asked, twirling the cup slowly between his fingers to cool it.

"Worse'n that. He wants my whole damned place."

"Got real big ideas."

"Plenty big. Bill Teague wants to own the county! Damn near does, excepting for my spread and a panhandle of brakes to the south of me."

Ryker took a swallow of the coffee, felt it jolt him. He stared wonderingly at the dark fluid. Medford chuckled.

"Reckon I forgot to tell you. Angus uses a fair amount of whiskey in his coffee making. Puts hair on it, he always says. We've sort of got used to it around here."

Jake took another pull at the cup. It was hot coffee-royal with the emphasis on the royal. He nodded appreciatively. "Does a man good," he said. Then, "Teague sure can't make you sell out if you don't want to."

"Maybe not, but he can drive me to the wall."

128

"How? You've got plenty of beef, all of it in prime shape."

"Just it. Got me a fine, big herd that's not doing me a whit of good because I can't sell off a single head. Got to just stand by and let them eat up good grass, get fat for nothing."

Curiously at ease now, Ryker finished off his cup, reached for the pot. "Don't savvy what you're getting at. Market for beef's plenty good, I hear."

The rancher drained his cup, refilled it, wagged his head. "It ain't that I don't want to sell my beef, or that I haven't tried," he said, settling back in his chair. "But — well, it's this way.

"Like I said, Teague's out to get my spread. The Box M is the only thing left around here he don't own, and it's setting right smack dab in the middle of everything that's his."

"Then he's bought up everything around you."

"Right. Bought if he had to, but just plain took, mostly. My ranch is sort of the key to it all, and with the lake that's on my west range —"

"Saw it. A body of water like that is a mighty fine sight in this part of the country."

"The Box M is something Teague's wanting in the worst way," Medford went on. "Tried to buy me out several times, Never was a real good offer, and never was too bad either. It's just that I ain't selling — not to him or nobody else. Hell, it took me a long time to build up to what I got and I'm not looking to turn it loose."

"Can understand. Money doesn't always count."

Medford smiled. "Ain't every man feels that way about it. Can see you do. Anyway, when Bill learned he wasn't going to yak me into a deal, he started forcing my hand — or trying to.

"Keeps hoorawing my hired help. I got less'n a dozen riders left. All the rest's been drove off by, scared by his bunch of hard cases. About ten men, that's all I've got, and me running better'n five thousand head of beef!"

"Five thousand!" Jake echoed, startled by the figures. "How can you —"

"Might as well be fifty," Medford cut in bitterly, "for all the good they're doing me. I'm flat broke — can't even meet wages."

"With all that stock and you're broke?"

"Can't sell a head. Teague's got me bottled up. No way of getting a herd to market. Tried this spring, three times. All it got me was about a hundred steers slaughtered and some of my cowhands shot up."

Jake Ryker considered the rancher's words in silence. He found it hard to believe that such could happen. "Seems there ought to be a way."

"You don't know Bill Teague. He'll stop at nothing. Besides carrying all the politicians in the county around in his hip pocket, he's got the hired help — guns — to do what he wants. Expect there's thirty, maybe forty men riding for him. Fixes it so's he can keep a tight ring around me day and night."

"Didn't see anybody when I came in other'n those three men of yours."

"Some of Teague's bunch spotted you. You can be sure of that. Where'd you ride in from?"

"Came down the Taladega Trail, then cut across country. Not too sure just where it was."

"Be northwest of here. They seen you. Didn't give you no trouble since they figured you was just some pilgrim headed east. Where'd you say you was going?"

"The Brazos. Park Justin's ranch. Know him?"

"Heard of him, never met him. Got hisself a big outfit, I'm told."

"Never met the man either," Ryker said, downing the last of his second cup of coffee. He felt much improved, but the need for sleep was beginning to tell on him now.

Medford took up the enameled pot, glanced at Jake. Ryker shook his head, watched the rancher pour his third helping.

"Figured to be big once myself," the rancher said absently. "Reckon all men get the notion somewheres along the line, but most of them get it knocked out of them like me. Teague's got me crowded up to where I'm caught between a hole and a high place, and can't move. Got a mortgage note to meet and hired hands to pay, along with regular expenses always hanging over my head. It turns out I can't meet any of them, I'm done for."

"Shame. You've got a fine place."

Medford's thin shoulders sagged helplessly. "Man can sure do a heap of hard work then have it end up meaning pure nothing. Like pouring sand into a rat hole — gets a fellow nowheres. Heard you say you and your brother had a ranch on the Pecos; you sell out?"

132

"No. We're sort of partners, but he does the ranching."

Medford paused, cup halfway to his lips. "I see. Somehow got the idea you was headed for Justin's to hire on."

"No, aimed to buy some cattle."

Medford drew himself up slowly. His eyes were bright as he set the cup back onto the dusty table.

"Buy cattle!" he echoed. "Hell-a-mighty, Ryker, I can sell you cattle — all you want! Don't know what you figured to pay Justin for beef, but I'll let you have all you want for eight dollars a head!"

XIV

"Eight dollars —" Jake murmured thoughtfully.

Medford pulled forward, came half out of his chair. His weathered face was eager, reflected the hope that now coursed through him.

"All right then — seven dollars!" The rancher was grasping frantically at straws that would save him from sinking into ruin.

Methodically Jake Ryker did some calculating. At seven dollars a head he could buy almost three hundred steers, a third more than he and Tom had planned on. If pushed, Medford would probably make a deal on that basis, but he'd not press the rancher to do so; he was never one to take advantage of a man when he was in a tight. Regardless, the extra cattle would be a big boost for the Circle R.

There was another advantage to consider, too; he'd be spared the long, dangerous drive from the Brazos, thus cutting down the chances of loss and putting him

134

back on the Pecos a lot sooner than he'd figured.

If he could get back at all.

That sobering thought clouded the bright vision from his mind. That was the catch — the whole problem; Bill Teague and his small army of hard cases had Medford pinned down — what made him think they'd let him drive three hundred steers off Box M range?

"What d'you say?" Medford asked tensely.

"A plenty good offer, but —"

"How much was you aiming to spend?"

"Two thousand —"

"Two thousand!" Medford repeated, sucking in his breath. "All right, tell you what — I'll give three hundred head, your pick or mine, range count or book tally, whichever. I'm ready for any kind of a deal you name."

Three hundred head for the same money Tom had intended to lay out for two hundred; and a drive that would be weeks shorter. It wouldn't matter to Park Justin, he was certain. A man doing as much business as he wouldn't miss the sale; likely he'd forgotten all about Tom Ryker and the Circle R by now.

"It a deal?" Medford asked anxiously.

135

Jake Ryker shrugged. Best to play it safe. There was too much at stake, and if things went wrong Callie and Tom would believe only that he had been careless and irresponsible and let them down. They'd never consider what the rewards of it would have been if he had come through.

"Like to take you up on it, but I don't see as I'd have any better luck driving a herd off your range than you've had."

Medford seemed to collapse. His shoulders went down and he settled back in his chair in defeat. "Well, maybe not. Could be Teague wouldn't bother you, them being your cattle and such. You'll be carrying a bill of sale, saying so."

"He'd know I bought them from you, and it'd be all the same to him — you selling cattle. Good offer, though; one I'd sure jump at if it was only me concerned. Way it is, however, I've got to play it safe."

Medford began to toy with the tips of his mustache. "Sure could use that two thousand," he mused. "Just ought to be a way somehow . . . You're looking to buy cattle, and I'm needing to sell. Got to be a answer somewheres."

Rising, the rancher moved to the edge of the gallery, stood there staring out into the sun-baked yard. Ryker, turned restless and fighting sleep, rose to his feet. Getting three hundred steers for what he intended to pay for two hundred would have really put the ranch on top, but there was no use hashing it over; he'd be a fool to gamble with the cards stacked the way they were.

"Real sorry," he said, stepping up beside Medford. "Wish there was some way. You mind if I drop over to your bunkhouse, grab myself about forty winks? Like to do some doctoring to my hurts, too, if it's all right with you."

"Sure — sure, go ahead," Medford answered, and then glanced up at the sudden rap of a horse entering the hard pack at a lope. "Hold on a minute," he said, as if struck with second thought. Beckoning to the rider, he yelled: "Max! Come over here for a minute!"

The rider bucked his head in acknowledgment of the summons. Pulling up to a corral, he dismounted, crossed to the house in quick, short strides. A thin, tall, mustached man, he was somewhere in his forties, Jake guessed.

The rancher turned to him. "Ryker, like for you to meet my foreman, Max Cameron."

Cameron nodded in a brisk, curt way,

offered his hand. His eyes were small and coal black.

"Pleased to meet you, Ryker."

Jake said, "Same goes for me."

"Ryker's from over in New Mexico. Got a place on the Pecos. On his way to buy beef from that fellow Justin. I'm trying to sell him some of my stock only there's the problem of getting them by Teague and his bunch. You got any ideas on how he might move out three hundred head?"

Cameron folded his arms across his chest, studied the distant plain.

"Don't see how I'd have any better luck than you've had," Jake said. "Being mine wouldn't help none since they'd know the steers came from here. Couldn't fool Teague on that."

"Expect you're right," the foreman said, toying with his mustache. "Let's see now, you'd aim to drive them west. One thing, Teague'd never figure us to start a herd in that direction because there ain't nothing that way — no market, I mean. We always have to take the trails to the north and east."

"What's that got to do —"

"Not saying for certain," Cameron continued, "but seems to me the odds would be plenty good. Teague's boys don't pay no mind to the panhandle. You just might get through."

Medford's eyes had recovered their bright glow of hope.

"Why, sure. There's a danged good chance of it! Better'n a good chance, I'd say — just about a surefire cinch maybe."

Ryker listened, also hopeful, but yet chary. The possibility of losing the cattle, once purchased, was a deep worry in his mind.

"Can't afford to take a risk," he said. "Have to tell you plain out that getting that herd taken away from me would put the Circle R out of business fast."

"Won't be much of a risk — and a man's got to take a few chances now and then if he expects to get ahead in this world. Stay poorer'n a churchmouse if he don't."

Ryker shrugged. "Not afraid to gamble. Done plenty of it one way or another in my time. But this is different." He could have told of the bad luck that had befallen Tom and the shaky condition the ranch was in, and of his own position in the matter, but such was family business and none of theirs.

Cameron turned to face him. "I'm telling you straight, the odds will be better than good."

"Take something better than that, something stronger."

Medford sank back into his chair, weary, beaten. He stared at Cameron hopelessly. "Well, was a thought. I can't blame Ryker for being careful. Two thousand's a lot of money."

Cameron drew out his handkerchief, mopped at his face. "Think maybe I've got a plan that'll work," he said, not giving up.

Ryker considered the man narrowly. "It'll have to be a good one," he said flatly. "Else save your breath."

"What is it, Max?" Medford asked, this time not responding to the prod of hope.

"How many steers did you say we're talking about?"

"Three hundred."

The lean foreman bobbed his head. "That's good. Not a big bunch." Moving to the table, he pushed the empty cups and granite pot into a corner. Digging into a pocket, he produced a pencil and a folded piece of paper.

Turning up a clean side of the sheet, he flattened the creases and said, "Here, let me show you what I'm thinking."

Drawing a small circle on the paper, Cameron said, "Here's where we are now. Now, about five miles to the south of us is the panhandle. Lot of rocks and brush and arroyos, not much else. There's one big wash that cuts across the whole works. Peters out this side of the New Mexico border say, ten maybe twelve miles."

"Sure," Medford said, face drawn into a tight frown. "Apache Wash. You saying he could take the cattle through there?"

"At night," Cameron said, nodding.

Medford rose to this feet. "Down the wash at night to where it ends, then cross over to the border — by God, it'll work!"

Max Cameron smiled quietly, confidently. "I can just about guarantee that if he makes it to the end of the arroyo, he's in the clear."

"And moving the stock at night when nobody'll notice, ought to make that part for sure."

"Right. We could set things up for him. I'll have the crew drift three hundred head into that hollow north of the wash tomorrow morning, let them graze and bed down there in case any of Teague's crew just happen to be watching.

"They'd not get leery, just figure we were changing a part of the main herd, moving it on to different grass like we're always doing. Then, come midnight, Ryker could head them out. Moon's pretty bright this

141

time of the month; don't figure the stock'd give any trouble."

"Why, it'd be no chore a'tall!" the rancher exclaimed.

"Sure, the way I see it."

Jake Ryker rolled the proposed plan about in his mind. It sounded practical, and the odds did seem to favor getting through. He'd evidently be on the lower end of Medford's range, a portion that bordered on brakes and that the rancher did not ordinarily use, since it led to no particular point. It seemed to him Max Cameron's reasoning was sound; the Rocking T outfit wasn't likely to be paying any attention to that section of the Box M.

"If you do that — drive the steers to where Apache Wash begins — how far will it be to the New Mexico border?"

Cameron stroked his mustache again. "Well, I'd reckon it at thirty miles from where you'd start to the point where you'd cross out of Texas into New Mexico."

"But you'd reach the end of the wash in about eighteen or twenty miles," Medford put in hurriedly. "You get there, you're safe. You wouldn't have to worry about nobody. Teague's bunch never rides that far south. Not his property for one thing — mainly because he don't want it; and there ain't nobody in that part of the country, for another."

"Something else," Cameron said, adding to the reassurances his boss was outlining, "if somebody spied the dust after it's daylight, they wouldn't think nothing about it. By that time you'd be a far piece from here and they'd just figure it was dust devils blowing across the mesa."

Jake Ryker rubbed at his chin, his mouth, weighed the problem: its advantages against the risks that he'd be taking. It was well worth the gamble he decided abruptly.

"All right," he said. "If you'll get me three hundred head down into that swale, like you said, you've got a deal."

XV

"That's good — that's good!" Medford exclaimed, thrusting out his hand. "You're showing sense. Ain't but once in a lifetime a man comes across the kind of bargain I'm giving you."

Quiet, Jake took the rancher's hand, sealed the deal. Now that the decision was made, he felt better. It would be risky, he was not overlooking that — but so was any trail drive. He could lose cattle, the whole herd, in fact, on a long drive such as he would face if he bought cattle from Park Justin — violent storms, raiders, wolves — a half a dozen or more similar possibilities.

It seemed to him he'd be taking no greater chance slipping through Bill Teague's blockade of the Box M than he would be assuming on a two hundred and fifty mile march, and the payoff would be much greater: a hundred fine, fat steers, to be exact. But he had to make it through. If he failed — Jake shook his head thoughtfully as he realized what Callie and Tom would say and believe should he fail.

144

It wouldn't be easy. He'd need to be on guard every moment of the time until he was across the line into New Mexico — even for a while after that.

"Expecting you to keep this quiet," he said then, turning to Medford and his foreman. "Get some of your crew to move the stock into that swale, way you planned. Let everybody, including your own hired hands, think it's just a regular —"

"I'll handle it," Cameron cut in coolly. "They won't ask questions. If they do, they won't get answers — none that'll tip them off to what you're doing, anyway."

Medford rubbed his palms together, frowned. "We able to spare a couple of men to help him make the drive?"

"Best I don't use any of your riders," Ryker said before Cameron could reply. "Be less chance of word leaking out, but mostly, if I'm spotted by any of the Rocking T crowd, I might have a better chance of talking my way through them if they don't see any of your men."

Medford nodded. "You're right. They could just leave you alone. But you sure can't drive three hundred head by yourself."

"Don't figure to try. There a town near here?"

"Closest is ten miles or so southeast. Place they call Polvareda."

"Teague's bunch hang out there?"

"Not much. Nothing to the dump. Cowhands usually do their drinking and womaning in Rock City, twenty miles north. Bigger town."

"Polvareda'll do fine," Ryker said.

"Best I tell you it's a Mex settlement."

"That's all right."

"You speak the lingo?"

"Pretty good. Cook my pa had — and my brother's still got — brought me up on it. Can usually get by with no trouble. We all understood now? Herd'll be in that hollow at the head of the wash and ready for me to move it out at tomorrow midnight?"

"Three hundred — they'll be there," Cameron said.

The rancher nodded his affirmative, brushed at his sweating face. "The two thousand, you're aiming to pay in cash, I take it?"

"In cash," Jake said. "When I take over the herd I'll have the money ready. Like that bill of sale then."

The rancher bobbed his head. "It'll be waiting for you." He paused, smiled apologetically. "It ain't that I'm mistrusting you,

146

son, just want to keep things on a pure business basis . . . Now, about tonight; you're welcome to bunk in with me."

Ryker said: "Obliged to you. Expect I'll take you up on the offer, but could be I'll be getting back late from this Polvareda. One thing I forgot to mention; I'll be needing two or three pack horses."

"Something I got plenty of, too," Medford said. "I'll throw them in on the deal for ten dollars each. Can scrape up enough grub to get you to the next town, too, if you like. Know you'll be wanting to travel light but there's a few things you'll have to have."

"Be a help. Once I get the herd over the line there won't be such a push."

"Just you leave it to me," the rancher said. "You go scare yourself up a crew, I'll look after everything else: grub, horses, water — the whole passel."

Ryker hesitated. He had only a few dollars of his own, and as far as he knew the belt contained an even two thousand cash, and no more.

"Little problem of money to pay for all that —"

Medford dismissed the objection with an airy wave of his hand. "Owe me! I'm beholden to you for buying some of my

147

beef. No reason why I can't show it by trusting you for a few dollars."

Jake grinned. Doing business with Medford was a real pleasure; there was no limit to his accommodation.

"You'll get your money soon as I'm back on the ranch," he said. "Now, if it's all right with you, I'll go over to your bunkhouse, clean myself up a bit. Could be I'll grab a couple hours sleep; then I'll ride over to Polvareda."

"Place is yours," Medford said. "Anything you need, just holler."

Jake Ryker, much improved after cleaning up, eating, submitting to the cook's medical ministrations, and a nap, mounted the chestnut around mid-afternoon and struck out along the road that bore into the southeast.

Within a short time, he rounded a low butte and sank into a broad valley through which a stream cut a crooked, shining path. Not long after that, he arrived at a cluster of trees growing in one of the creek's wider bends and there saw the scatter of two dozen or so squat adobe huts and buildings that made up the settlement of Polvareda.

The single street — actually a lengthy

148

patio along which the structures were arranged — was silent and deserted when he turned into it. In a sweeping glance, Ryker took in the plain huts, the one saloon with the sign CANTINA canted above the door; the tiny Catholic church and its adjacent, fenced in cemetery, the single store that served as a supply point for all the inhabitants' needs.

Ignoring the two or three mongrel dogs that came forth finally from the shade alongside the houses to challenge his appearance, he pulled to a halt underneath a spreading cottonwood that grew in the center of the village. There was the smell of cooking chili on the still air, and that stirred a recollection of his childhood, when old Cocinero kept a quantity of the biting peppers continually cooking on his stove and filling the yard with their fragrance.

The dogs tired, slunk off into the weeds. The place appeared to have been abandoned, but Ryker knew such was far from the truth; he was being observed by many pairs of eyes, some curious, some suspicious, others fearful. Americans — *gringos* — weren't particularly welcome in such villages. Best course to follow was to take it slow and easy. Sooner or later someone would come into the open. Patience, he'd learned from Cocinero, was a prized facet of the Mexican personality, almost a way of life, in fact.

Response came more quickly than he had anticipated. A boy, twelve or possibly fourteen years of age, wearing worn but clean cotton shirt and pants, eased through the doorway of the hut immediately opposite the big cottonwood, watched him silently.

Ryker swung off the chestnut, smiled at the youngster. *"Hola, muchacho! Que tal?"* he said, mustering his Spanish.

The boy remained impassive to the greeting for several moments. Finally, he sauntered disinterestedly into the street, brown face tipped down shyly.

"I am in search of riders who can drive cattle," Jake said. "Do you know of any?"

The boy looked up, frowned. After a bit, he said, "There are some. I do not know if they wish to work."

"I will pay in gold."

The boy's dark eyes brightened. "This work, it is near the village?"

"Partly. Also in New Mexico. A man would be gone from his house for a time of seven days perhaps. I will pay twenty dollars gold for such."

150

The young Mexican drew to sharp attention at that. His features became serious. "There are those who may accept such work. I for one."

Jake smiled. "You are but a boy —"

"But strong. Often I have done the labor of a man."

"There could be danger."

The boy shrugged. "When is there not? I have no fear."

"Such may well be. These men of whom you speak, where will I find them?"

"I can take you to them, but first I must know for myself; is there work for me also?"

Ryker mopped at the sweat on his face, grinned. He was being neatly blackmailed and knew it. He nodded. "Your name?"

"Miguel Calderon."

"Very well, Miguel Calderon. If your mother and father will permit it, you have a job."

"It is my mother we must speak of. My father is dead by the church."

"I understand. We will talk with her, but first take me to where I can speak with these men."

Miguel wheeled and led the way to a small building behind the general store.

151

"Aqui este el ayuntamiento," he said, pointing.

The word was not familiar to Ryker. He rubbed at his jaw. "I do not understand."

"The house where there are meetings," the boy explained.

A town hall, Jake realized. "Is there a meeting now?"

"The men gather there each day to talk and drink wine when there is no work in the fields or other places to be found. Some will be there. Blas Armijo — he is one with much experience where there are cattle — you will find him. He is always there. My mother says he drinks too much wine."

One *vaquero.* That was fortunate, assuming he was sober, could remain so and was willing to work. Ryker felt the boy's sharp, brown eyes drilling into him.

"Will you not enter?"

"If it is permitted."

"I shall go with you. Such will make it all right."

Miguel crossed over to the deep inset door, opened it and stepped inside. Jake followed more slowly, hearing the bantering greeting the boy's appearance evoked.

"A man of tender years," a voice called

jokingly. "Does he seek to tip the skin of wine with us?"

"Perhaps he desires something of greater strength," another remarked.

Miguel squared his slight shoulders. "I come with a friend — one who wishes to pay gold for a short time of work in New Mexico."

There was a faint scuffling sound in the murky depths of the room. A door was opened in a back wall and a band of daylight broke across the darkness. Ryker could see a half a dozen men squatting about, backs to the mud brick walls. Most were too old for the job he had to offer.

Spurs jingled. A moment later a lean, middle-aged Mexican dressed in the full regalia of a *vaquero* moved up to the entrance.

"You are welcome here," he said to Ryker, and bowed slightly.

Jake entered, halted. There was a table at the opposite end of the dirt-floored room. A few benches were placed here and there. All were being ignored for the more informal habit of squatting on the heels.

The *vaquero* — Blas Armijo the boy had called him — handed Ryker the skin of wine, again inclined his head. "We are honored to have you share our wine."

Jake could detect the faint thread of irony in the man's tone, the tinge of patronizing mockery. He ignored it.

"The honor is mine," he said, and tipped the vessel to his lips. The wine had a tart, fruity taste, burned somewhat on its downward passage.

Passing the liquor back to Armijo, he said, "Many thanks," and waited. The matter of business would come in due time. It had been mentioned. It would be impolite for him to bring it up again.

"You have come from New Mexico?" an elderly man puffing on a limp, brown cigarette asked.

"From the Pecos River country."

"Once I was through there," the old one mused. "It was in the days when I often journeyed to Santa Fe. Ah, Santa Fe — it does well?"

Ryker had not visited the ancient capital in years but little ever changed there, he knew. "It does well," he assured the man.

Armijo leaned against the door's thick frame, struck a match to a slim cigar. "This work of which you speak, it has to do with cattle?"

Ryker nodded. "Yes. I have a small herd of three hundred I wish to drive to the ranch of my brother and me in New

Mexico. It will require three men of experience — and Miguel here, whom I have already hired."

There was a moment of quiet laughter during which the boy shifted self-consciously.

"For the work I will pay twenty dollars in gold. Food will also be furnished."

"It is fair," the *vaquero* said. "When will this drive begin and from where will it start?"

"I wish those who agree to meet me at the arroyo to the south of the Medford ranch. At sundown."

"The place is well known to us all. It is called the Arroyo of the Apaches. Once there was a fierce battle with the Indians there."

Ryker nodded to the elderly speaker. Medford and Cameron had mentioned the name, he had neglected to quote it. He said nothing of that, however, simply bowed slightly to the old man, said, "Thank you, Uncle," and turned his attention again on Blas Armijo.

"It is settled? I can expect three men at the arroyo at sundown tomorrow?"

"It is agreed," the *vaquero* replied. "I myself shall be there with two others of reliable character."

XVI

Ryker backed into the open, beckoned for the *vaquero* to follow. Armijo complied quickly, with Miguel trailing behind.

"There is something?" Armijo asked.

Jake said: "A matter of importance to me. It will be wise to say nothing of this to others. Also, it will be a favor if you will caution the men inside to not speak of it."

Blas Armijo's brows lifted. He leaned against the weather-washed adobe wall of the building, a spur making a clear, bell-like tinkling as he cocked one booted foot against its base.

"There is a secret that must be kept?"

"From certain persons. You know of the trouble that lies between the rancher Medford and another of the name Bill Teague?"

The *vaquero's* eyes glittered. "Who does not know of Bill Teague and his men. Also of the trouble. Such is not of a secret nature."

"True. The secret concerns me in that the cattle that are to be driven were purchased by me from Medford. Should Teague or his men learn of this fact, they will attempt to halt us and there will be trouble."

Armijo sucked at his slender cigar in thoughtful silence. Finally he stirred, said, "We have no wish to involve ourselves in the trouble of these two men. Teague is one who is no friend of the Mexican people. Nor are his riders. And since we are but a small village and few in number, it is wise for us to not have them as enemies."

"I hope to avoid trouble. The plan I shall follow is such that we will not encounter any of the man's riders unless ill luck befalls us."

Again Blas Armijo's features were solemn in thought. "An encounter would then be only in the nature of an accident? There is small chance such will occur?"

"A very small one, greatly lessened if word of the drive is not spread. We shall take a route that Teague's men do not frequent, most of which will be traveled at night. I have faith there will be no incidents."

"Very well," the *vaquero* said in his stiff, formal way. "The others will be warned. We have no love for this Teague and those

157

who work for him. It will be an honor and privilege to partake of a venture that reduces him in stature."

Ryker extended his hand. "I thus have your word that caution will be used and that you, with two good men, will be at the Apache Wash tomorrow at sunset to begin the drive?"

"It is true," Armijo assured him, closing his slim fingers around those of Ryker.

"Good. It is settled. Until later."

"Go with God," the *vaquero* murmured, and turned to reenter the building.

Jake dropped his hand on Miguel's shoulder. "We must now speak with your mother, young one."

The boy looked up at him, worry in his eyes. "You will say little to her of this man Teague?"

"How can it be avoided? She must be made aware of the possibility of trouble."

"But if she believes the work to be dangerous she will oppose my going."

"Perhaps, but it is always wise to be honest, especially with one's elders."

Miguel's shoulders drooped. "Very well," he said disconsolately, "but I shall go whether she wishes it or not."

Silent, he led the way through the late afternoon sunlight to the hut where he

158

lived. Jake trailed him through the low doorway, noting the caged mockingbird near a window as he stepped into the cool interior created by the thick walls, noting also the few furnishings and the utter cleanliness of everything.

"Mama!" the boy called, halting in the last of the three rooms strung end to end: parlor, bedroom and kitchen; identical to the shotgun shanties of many homesteaders.

"Here —"

Her reply came from the yard. Ryker followed the boy into the open where a woman somewhere near his own age was removing wash from a clothesline stretched between two trees. She was light-skinned for her race, but she had the shining black hair and large, doe-soft brown eyes that distinguished her kind.

When her gaze fell upon Ryker she straightened, the stiffness of fear coming into her manner. Dropping the cloth she was holding into the reed basket at her feet, she straightened her black cotton skirt, tugged briefly at the collar of the white shirtwaist she was wearing, and stepped forward.

"There is trouble, Miguel?"

"No, no Mama!" the boy replied indig-

159

nantly. "This gentleman wishes to give me work. He will tell you of it."

Relief came into the woman's features. She moved nearer. Late afternoon sunlight caught at the coil of jet strands on the nape of her neck glinted softly.

"I am Maria Calderon," she said smiling, and offered her hand.

"My name is Ryker," Jake replied, introducing himself and giving her firm, work worn hand the single pumping motion customary with the Mexican people. "It is a pleasure to know Miguel's mother. He is a fine boy."

"Thank you. This work you have for him?"

"I am driving a herd of cattle from a place near here to the ranch of my brother and myself in New Mexico —"

"He will be taken from here?" Maria broke in, her features filling with alarm.

"Yes. The work will require a few days of absence. A week perhaps."

"I shall be paid twenty dollars in gold, Mama!" the boy said excitedly. "So much money!"

"It is a small fortune," Maria agreed, not taking her eyes off Ryker. "Why do you wish for him to accompany you? He is hardly of an age for such a —"

"I can do a man's work," Miguel protested, seeking to head off her objection. "Have I not done so before? This will not be hard for me, this riding of a horse and driving cattle."

The woman continued to study Jake, awaiting his answer to her question. He smiled. "It is that he asked and is one of considerable persistence. I had promised."

Maria nodded, smiled also. "Of this I am aware." Her manner relented. "I suppose there is no harm in it . . . a cattle drive. Are there others from Polvareda who are to work with you?"

"Blas Armijo. He is also to find two more men. There will be four of us, and Miguel."

At the mention of the *vaquero's* name Maria Calderon's nose crinkled slightly in disapproval, but she made no comment.

"I must tell you there is a possibility of trouble, but only a small possibility. I shall watch the boy carefully and protect him from harm if it is in my power to do so. This can also be expected of Blas Armijo, I am sure."

Again Maria frowned. "I — I do not know. He is so young, and I have nothing else — no one."

"I am the man of the household,"

161

Miguel stated soberly. "It is right that I do the things that are expected of me."

"Of course —"

"Can we not use the twenty dollars in gold?"

Maria smiled then, showing her strong, white teeth. "Very well, it shall be. As you have said, it is only right." She turned to Jake. "I thank you for what you do."

"For nothing," Ryker said. "I am pleased to help, but he will work just as the others. He will receive no favors except if there be trouble."

"That is as it should be. He will take his place with the men, then he must be treated the same as the men. When is it you leave?"

"Tomorrow night. From the place they call Apache Wash."

Maria Calderon nodded slowly. "My grandfather was slain there in a terrible battle with the Indians," she murmured. "Could such have evil portent for Miguel?"

"I think not," Ryker replied and glanced to the boy. "I will have a horse there awaiting you. Is it possible for you to ride with one of the others to the place?"

"Blas will take me with him behind his saddle," Miguel said confidently.

"Good. Then I shall see you at the proper time. Now, I must go."

Maria Calderon's face clouded immediately. "You will not stay for the evening meal with us? It is late, and I note that you have been injured."

Only a woman would have commented on the presence of his bandages, Ryker thought. None of the men, although the white strips of cloth on his head and arm were unavoidably noticeable, had said anything. It was their way, for to have inquired would have been considered probing and therefore impolite. But a woman's way was different; one of genuine concern and heartfelt sympathy.

"The injuries are nothing," he assured her, "and while I would be honored to take the meal with you and Miguel, I must return at once. There is much that I have yet to do. There will be another time, perhaps?"

"Our house is your house," Maria said. "You are welcome at all times. Good-bye."

"Adiós," he replied, echoing the gentle farewell.

Returning to the chestnut, he swung onto the saddle and cut around, headed back for Medford's. He was hungry but he had not wanted to impose on Maria

163

Calderon's hospitality, knowing well that for them food was not always easy to come by. To have offered to help would have been an unpardonable insult; accordingly, to decline was the only course open to him. If he hurried, he probably would make it to Medford's in time to eat with the crew.

And he could get back to talking in plain English again. He was weary of the prim, formal manner in which he'd been required to speak, of the polite fencing, of being careful to observe all the amenities so dear to the Mexican people. He respected their customs and their courteous mannerisms, even admired them, but that hour or so in Polvareda had called for more Spanish than he'd spoken in years, and the effort had drained him bone dry.

XVII

There were three hundred and five head in the herd, Medford tossing in the five extra, when they turned up in the tallying, for good luck, which he said he was sure Jake would have.

Ryker, fingering the bill of sale he had received at the conclusion of the transaction, watched the rancher and Max Cameron ride off, taking with them the cowhands who had brought in the cattle. The full realization of the responsibility that he now shouldered drove home to him at that point, and for several long, lonely moments he stood there staring at the departing horsemen.

He had given over the two thousand dollars Tom had entrusted to him, and he had a fine herd of cattle to show for the money. He should have no qualms. In times past he had handled larger sums of cash, managed herds of greater number. But this was different. He supposed it was the fact that Tom and Callie were depending upon him — that they had done so reluctantly and

165

with little faith in his ability to come through.

A bit of impatience stirred him. Hell, money was only money, cattle only cattle, and while he didn't expect it, anybody could have bad luck, run into trouble . . . Only, he couldn't let that happen. He had to get the herd to the Circle R, come tornado or taxes — and then he'd be through.

He wasn't cut out for this sort of life: all the strain and worry and sweating out the possibility of losing money, of mothering a bunch of steers and keeping them alive for the sake of his own self and kin. Where someone else was concerned it was different; they recognized his ability and never doubted his integrity, and he was free to come and go as he pleased. He'd do what he'd decided earlier, find a good man for a foreman, and then take off.

But first he had to get the herd to the Circle R. It was all up to him now. He could not fall back on Medford or Cameron for help, and there was no turning back and canceling out the deal to recover the two thousand. It was the same as having walked out onto quicksand. He could do nothing but go on, try to reach the opposite side.

Tucking the ownership paper in his

pocket, he glanced to the horizon in the west. The sun was gone, and now a flare of gold was spraying into the steel blue of the sky, touching the bellies of the scattered clouds and setting them afire.

It would be dark in another hour. He'd start the herd moving then. No sense holding off until midnight. The herd had loafed, grazed and watered in the swale all that day. They wouldn't be difficult to handle, and two or three more hours on the trail during the night could spell the difference in avoiding trouble or encountering it.

Touching the chestnut with his spurs, Ryker moved forward, swinging along the west side of the bedded down cattle. Blas Armijo and the two men he'd recruited to help, Oreste and Tiofilo Luna, brothers, and young Miguel were already on the job, drifting quietly about the fringes of the herd.

The *vaquero* was keening softly in a low voice, and twice Jake had seen him reach into the ornately decorated leather pocket of his big Mexican saddle, procure a bottle and have a swallow of its contents. So far the liquor seemed to be having no effect on him; until it did, he'd say nothing to the man about it.

Miguel, overwhelmed by the pony and

167

gear Ryker had provided, was being careful to do all things right, listening attentively to the instructions Armijo gave him and carrying them out with the alacrity and enthusiasm of youth. Each time Jake caught his eye the boy responded with a wide grin.

Medford had made it easy. When the final moment came for passing over the cash in exchange for the herd and the bill of sale covering it, the rancher had produced also three pack mules loaded with trail grub and water as well as a quantity of grain for the horses to keep them in good condition for the trip.

Ryker had gone to some pains personally, however, in selecting a mount and gear for Miguel, insisting that the rancher add it to what he owed for the mules and the supplies. A boy trying to take the place of a father deserved encouragement and reward, he felt.

Coming to the far end of the herd, Jake crossed over to where Blas sat, one leg hooked around the horn of his hull, smoking one of the thin, black cigars of which he seemed to have an inexhaustible supply.

"Soon as it's full dark, we'll move them out," he said.

The *vaquero* nodded. "I have note there is a leader steer," he said, also using English. "Oreste has taken him to the front. The others will follow."

That was good news. Ryker raised himself in the stirrups, looked to the forward line of cattle. He located the longhorned, old brindle standing spraddle legged and somewhat belligerently apart from the rest.

"Fine. Once we get him headed down the wash we shouldn't have too much trouble. Oreste and Tiofilo — have they driven cattle before?"

"There have been times," Armijo said, lapsing into his more easily managed native tongue. "They are good men. They will do as directed." He paused, turned his eyes to where Miguel was walking his pony slowly along the edge of the herd. "The young one, he will be a man, eh?"

"A good one," Ryker said, "but no harm must come to him." He roweled the gelding into motion. "I will give the signal when it is time. Also, it is best that all things be done quietly once the drive has begun."

"Agreed."

Jake rode on. The *vaquero* was armed, he saw, and was relieved to know that. If something developed there would be at least two guns among them. Neither Oreste nor his brother, nor, of course, Miguel had a weapon.

He glanced again at the west. The gold flare had paled to a thin yellow and the cottony clouds no longer were tipped with color. Long fingers of shadow were beginning to creep across the land, and in the deeper recesses of the wash where flash floods had in times past gouged great handfuls of the red soil, pockets of blackness had formed.

A pearl-like haze was settling over the country. Overhead, a gaggle of crows were cutting their way through the sky, headed, no doubt, for the trees around Medford's and the easy pickings they would find around the corrals and barn. Somewhere in the stillness a cock quail gave his sharp, quick call.

Things would be starting to stir in the saloons and gambling halls of the big trail towns — Abilene, Wichita, Fort Worth, Dodge and all the others. They would have the big hanging lamps lit, and the soft, yellow glow would be seeking out the corners of the rooms, tinting the skins of the drovers and cowhands and gamblers and such frequenters who came within range of their flare, and shining on the bangles of the saloon girls' dresses.

The good smell of smoke would be everywhere, blending subtly with the stale, but still friendly odor of spilled whiskey and beer and the plain, everyday stink of sweat and dust. An undercurrent of excitement would be threading the crowds, further heightened, perhaps, by the sudden tenseness of a threatened gunfight over the turn of a card, a misspoken word, or possibly the smile of a woman.

And there were those nights on the trail . . . A man was a king then, alone but never lonesome, hunched over a fire on some high plain, or deep in a quiet, warm valley while hardtack and bacon heated and sizzled over the flames to the accompaniment of gently bubbling coffee.

In that way of life a man wanted for little, needed but little; a good horse, strong tack, a few trail conveniences — spider, coffee can and cup — and a few dollars now and then to buy grub and an occasional drink or play a few hands of poker. True, it was a road that led nowhere if calculated on the basis of worldly possessions and accomplishments, but the importance of that was a matter of opinion; one involving the question of values and just what constituted the greatest worth.

For himself, Jake Ryker was sure he knew what was more important to him; simply being a man among men, free to come and go as he willed in a life uncomplicated by possessions and firm attachments, while he reveled in the appreciation and enjoyment of simply being alive in a world of matchless grandeur and beauty.

That was where he and Tom differed so vastly. To the older Ryker security was what counted most; a consideration Jake never wasted a moment's worry over. It had always been that way, and that bridgeless gap between them was one that would never close. Jake knew that, and while he regretted it for the sake of blood ties, it caused him no loss of sleep.

He was glad of one thing, however; the extra hundred steers he was bringing back to the Circle R should cause Tom and Callie to feel their future was a much better one.

He swung away from the herd, loped the chestnut to the crest of a nearby hill. Halting, he swept the darkening country with a probing gaze. There was no sign of riders anywhere. Only the scurrying about of a family of gophers in a ravine to his left broke the absolute, inert quality of the surroundings. So far they had not drawn any attention from Bill Teague's men.

He cut back, dropped off the short slope and angled toward Blas Armijo, still taking his ease on the slim-legged bay horse he rode.

"Move 'em out," he called in a low voice.

The *vaquero* bobbed his head, flipped his stump of a cigar away and dropped his leg into place. Roweling his mount with the big star spurs he wore, he wheeled off, slanting for the front of the herd. Ryker heard him sing out in a guarded voice to the Luna brothers, and turned away, doubling back for the rear of the herd. Looking over his shoulder he saw the men riding in among the cattle, flaying about with their rawhide lariats.

Jake, with Miguel suddenly close by, followed the same procedure, and shortly, with the first shine of the moon silvering the landscape, the steers were up and moving sluggishly down the wash.

An hour later, with the old brindle in charge, the herd had strung out into a compact, narrow oblong that flowed steadily within the banks of Apache Wash. It was accomplished much more easily than anticipated, and Jake guessed he

173

could thank Medford and Max Cameron for that; the cattle had rested for almost a full day and were far from tired. As a result, their customary reluctance to travel after sundown was greatly minimized.

Leaving the Lunas to ride drag, Miguel and the *vaquero* at flank positions, and relying upon the lead steer to follow the course of the arroyo, Ryker pulled away from the herd, began a constant circling of it at a distance, while he maintained a watch for riders appearing in the night.

The dust lifted by the plodding hooves turned dark and heavy, began to hang like a threatening cloud over the wash. By day it certainly would have been noticed from a considerable distance; in the light of the stars and moon it would go unseen except at close range. He owed Max Cameron his appreciation for that idea, too; that of a night drive through the arroyo.

The herd moved on steadily, and as the hours passed the miles melted away. Apache Wash, Jake recalled, was somewhere in the neighborhood of twenty miles long, a bit less, possibly. He couldn't hope to cover the entire distance before sunrise, of course, but at the pace they were traveling, they would not fall too far short.

All they need do was reach the end of

174

the arroyo safely and they'd have half the job done insofar as Bill Teague's riders were concerned, Medford and his foreman had assured him.

The wash deepened, narrowed, became a brush-cluttered gorge. A short time later it widened again, lifted toward the level of the surrounding plain. Loose sand slowed the pace, rock-studded ground increased it. The sky to the east began to gray, the earth formations and growths which were mysterious, unfamiliar silhouettes in the night, took shape, lost their enigma. Jake veered into the herd, sought out Blas Armijo.

The *vaquero* met him with a broad grin. "It goes well this cattle drive, eh?"

Ryker nodded. "Couldn't ask for anything better. Going to be daylight soon. Any idea how far it is yet to the end of the arroyo?"

Armijo shrugged. "Five miles, perhaps less."

They'd fall that much short of making it out of Apache Wash by sunup. It couldn't be helped. He'd hoped to be nearer than that but a herd travels just so fast, and he had to admit they had done better than usual.

"We do not stop?" the *vaquero* asked.

175

"There is a place of wideness not far. Possibly one hour from now."

Jake Ryker frowned, said, "Want to cover as much ground as we can before we pull up and camp. Nearer we are to the New Mexico border, the better I'll feel."

Blas glanced around, dark eyes sweeping the gradually lightening country. "There has been no one to follow?"

"Haven't spotted anybody. If Teague's bunch are onto us, they're keeping out of sight."

"Such cannot be so. There is little place on this prairie land to hide except in this wash — and we are there."

The *vaquero* produced one of his cigars, offered it to Jake. When the tall redhead declined, he bit off the tapered end, spat it aside and thumbed a match into a small flame. Puffing the weed into life, he jerked his head in the direction of the herd.

"They will go two, maybe three hours more. Then they will wish to stop. There will be no driving them for they will be tired and stubborn. And there is no water for their thirst."

"Know that, but the worst of it will be behind us. From what Medford told me, there's water on the other side of the border."

"Yes, a small place of water provided by a windmill. It will take much time and labor to water the cattle there."

"Only place we'll hit before we reach the Pecos, unless you know of another."

"I do not."

"Then we'll have to make it do. But that's something we'll worry about when the time comes."

A hollow, flat crack echoed through the dust haze. Armijo, holding his cigar by thumb and forefinger, suddenly released it. A look of puzzlement crossed his swarthy features. Ryker stared at the man, and then, as a red stain began to spread down the front of the *vaquero's* shirt, he realized that Blas Armijo had been shot, that the sound he had heard was the report of a rifle.

"*Señor* —" the *vaquero* murmured, raising a hand. "*Yo*—"

Abruptly, he fell forward, toppled from his saddle. More rifle shots began to pop through the racket of the suddenly running herd. A bullet sang off Ryker's hull, another plucked at his arm. Galvanized into sudden action, he wheeled away, dragging out his pistol as he spurred for a rise to his left.

He could see no one through the hovering clouds of yellow dust, could only guess that the raiders, whoever they were, had come in from that side of the arroyo.

Cursing, he broke out into the clear, looked frantically around for Miguel, for the Luna brothers and the attackers. Two men were bearing down upon him at a fast gallop. One carried a handgun, the other a rifle. Likely he had been the marksman who had sighted in on Blas Armijo and picked him off.

Anger rising in him, Jake Ryker raised his weapon, snapped a bullet at the oncoming pair, and veered back into the pall. Miguel should be on the opposite side of the running herd. He would be fairly safe there unless more raiders were moving in from that quarter.

Grim, Jake crouched low over the saddle as the chestnut legged it for the farther side of the wash. Were these Teague's men, or had he run into a bunch of rustlers out to grab a small herd for themselves? It didn't matter; they meant to get what they came after and were not adverse to killing everybody who stood in their way.

Again he was out of the boiling dust. He saw two riders wheel off to his left, white clad figures flat on their saddles as they raced to gain the safety of the distant

178

brush. The Luna brothers. They were getting out of it fast. Unarmed, they had no other choice.

Miguel! Where the hell was Miguel?

Motion to one side caused him to swerve the chestnut. He tried to pierce the wall of shifting brown with squinting eyes. A horse broke into view, two more. Raiders! The pair he'd seen earlier, and another.

He threw two quick shots at them, spurred the gelding again into the sheltering curtain of dust, hearing the vicious chatter of rifles, the higher pitched crackle of pistols.

Miguel must have made a run for it, too, just as the Lunas did. He hoped so. There was nothing the boy could do but get himself hurt, Jake realized. It was best he face the outlaws alone, for the only thing that counted now was a gun. But Miguel . . . Worry and uneasiness plagued him. He must be sure the boy was safe first. He had to find him, had to be certain of it. Roweling the chestnut, he sent the big horse plunging ahead. One thing, if the cattle continued to run, his chances for saving them were good. But that really didn't matter. It was Miguel that counted. The hell with the cattle. Miguel —

Abruptly two riders loomed up in the

179

murk. Jake reflexed a shot even as he saw the pale flash of their weapons. In the next fleeting fragment of time the gelding veered hard right. Jake Ryker saw the broad, spreading horns of a confused steer directly in front of him, clawed at the saddle horn to save himself from falling.

XVIII

Ryker's fingers wrenched free of the saddle horn. He felt himself pitch forward and down. He struck hard. Pain surged through him, but the instinct to survive kept him conscious, drove him back to his feet. The herd was all around him, it seemed; bawling, heaving, wild-eyed steers cutting back and forth in the dust. Something hit him from behind. He went down again, endeavored to rise, and then, as force from a different angle smashed into him with a sickening impact, he lost all awareness.

It was cool and dark when he once more opened his eyes. Somewhere nearby a dog was barking and the air was clear and sweet and filled with the smell of simmering beans larded with pork. He shook off the haze that drifted loosely about in his brain, winced as the movement brought on a momentary onslaught of stabbing pain. He rode out several long minutes, then struggled to gain a sitting position. The best he could do was come to an elbow.

He was in a small, familiar room. A caged mockingbird in the deep-set window opposite his bunklike bed eyed him mistrustingly, and that, too, evoked a stir of remembrance. It came to him then. He was in the home of Maria and Miguel Calderon.

Fighting to organize his thoughts, he lay back, began to puzzle it out. There had been the raid; rustlers, or maybe they'd been Teague's men. Regardless, Blas Armijo had been killed, the Luna brothers had fled the scene and he had been thrown from his horse while searching for Miguel.

Relief registered on his mind. Evidently the boy was all right. Only Miguel could have brought him to the Calderon house after he'd been knocked out.

But the herd was lost — gone.

A bitter oath slipped from his lips as that fact broke through to him. Maybe, if he could get on his feet, go back to Apache Wash there'd still be a chance. Again he tried to rise. Curiously, he had no strength, and movement rewarded him only with pain. He relaxed, lifted a hand and touched the tightness that encircled his head. Either he'd taken another hard rap there or else the old wound had reopened, for a fresh bandage had been applied. He

182

noted then the strip of new, clean white about his arm. Evidently Maria had dressed both his injuries. There had been nothing she could do for the soreness that claimed his body, however. Every muscle and bone of his being was making itself known.

He swore again in a low, breathless way. It didn't matter. He had to get on his feet. He'd weather the pain somehow. Important thing was the herd — those raiders —

"You are awake."

Maria Calderon's voice greeted him from the doorway leading into the kitchen. Turning her head, she called into the yard: "Miguelito, he is awake!"

Ryker lay back, watched the woman come into the room, hearing at the same time the quick rush of footsteps across the hard-packed floor. A moment later the boy was standing in the room smiling at him through the dimness.

"You are well!" he exclaimed happily.

"Not well," Maria corrected. "It is only that he has returned from the unconsciousness given to him by the fall. Another day, perhaps two —"

"No!" The word sprang angrily from Ryker's lips. "I must find my cattle, recover them."

183

"That cannot be done so soon," Maria replied in her calm, quiet way. "If you will arise, you will learn that such is true."

Jake Ryker mustered his strength once more, sought to draw himself upright, failed. Frustration ripped through him again. There was no use trying to fool himself. He didn't have it in him.

"Now perhaps patience will come to you," the woman said. "Do you hunger?"

Ryker moved his head slightly, very carefully, replying that he did not. He reached out for Miguel's hand, wrapped it in his own. A quietness had moved into him now that he had accepted the situation.

"You were not injured, young friend?"

"No. I am well."

"Good. But the herd — it is gone?" He knew the answer without asking but he was hoping against the inevitable.

The boy nodded solemnly.

Jake Ryker was silent for a long minute, eye on the mockingbird. Then, "Did you see all that happened there in the arroyo? Part is known to me. Blas Armijo was shot and is dead. The Luna brothers escaped to the brush. I was riding with the herd seeking you when my horse was frightened by a steer that turned upon him. I remember falling but little of what took place after."

184

"I was safe," Miguel said. "Oreste called to me to hide by a small tree that was near when the shooting started. I saw the bandits ride among the herd. There were four of them, I think. Perhaps five."

"Were any known to you?"

"I do not think so. Possibly I have seen them, but there were none I can call by name."

"What of the Lunas? Did they return to the village?"

"No, it is thought they are hiding among the trees of the sand hills because they fear to return to their homes."

Ryker mulled that over. It could mean the brothers knew the identity of the raiders. It would pay to find them, ask questions.

"It was you who brought me to your home," Jake said then, coming back to the boy.

"Yes. It was near where I hid that you fell from your horse. I waited until the bandits were gone and went then to where you lay. There was much blood."

"Miguel did well," Maria said, a note of pride in her voice. "The wound in your head was bleeding. Also that in your arm. And you had many cuts and scratches. He stopped the flowing with his handkerchief.

185

What is of a mystery to me is how he was able to put you on your horse — he, one so small."

"I am strong for my size," the boy declared. "Also, it was with his own help. When I explain to him that he must rise to the saddle, the effort was made although I truly do not think he was awake entirely. Thus, with my help, it was done."

Jake could recall nothing of climbing back onto the chestnut, or of the ride back to Polvareda. He had managed it all instinctively, he supposed.

"I am in your debt, my young friend," he said, again grasping the boy's hand. "To you also, Mrs. Calderon." He glanced down at the clean clothing he wore: the change he had carried in his saddlebags. "It appears you not only took me in but also were kind enough to clean and dress me."

False modesty was no part of Maria Calderon. She shrugged, said matter-of-factly: "The clothing was torn in many places, covered also with blood and dust — as were you. It was necessary to remove the rags and bathe you, after which the clothing found with your saddle was used."

"Such was a great kindness. I hope no

trouble will befall you from the outlaws because of me."

Maria looked down. "It is to be hoped they will not search here for you."

Alarm shot through Ryker. "They search for me?"

"Yes."

"Then it is best I leave your house, find a different place to hide."

"Wait, hear it all. The men who went to recover the body of Blas Armijo encountered two of the bandits. They asked of you. It was hoped by them apparently that you were dead also, since that is what they wished. The men replied they knew nothing and the outlaws went away. It is not known if the information satisfied them or not."

Ryker frowned. "Likely they will come here for there will be those in the village who saw Miguel bring me to your house."

"Nothing will be said by them if questioned. There is no love among them for the *gringos*. Too long have they — we felt the point of their cruel ways."

There was a bitterness to Maria's words, and looking closely at the woman, Jake saw anger in her dark eyes.

"There are few in Polvareda who do not owe the one who worked for the ranchers a debt of hate," she continued. "Each would look forward to a means for repaying in kind the treatment they have received."

"I am sorry for what has happened to you," Ryker said. "But all of my people — all Americans — are not like those of whom you speak. Most respect the Mexicans and the Spaniards. There are bad apples in all barrels."

"This I know," Maria said, sighing. "It is that there are times when I am carried away by strong thoughts — by things I remember."

"Life will change for you, become good. You are deserving of such," Jake said, and added, "Do you think it would be possible to find Oreste and Tiofilo?"

Maria shrugged. "Perhaps. I think they will send word to their families, advise them of their hideout. You wish to speak with them?"

"Yes. It is of importance. I believe they may know the raiders by name. Such might bring about the recovery of my cattle. Unless I am able to do that, the loss will come as a great blow to my brother and his wife. And to me."

"I shall make inquiry," Maria said, glancing through the doorway into the dark. "If —"

"You must not do this," Miguel broke in anxiously. "If they search for our friend, it is possible they will find you. When it is late I will go and look for the cattle."

"You —" Ryker began protestingly.

"It will be a simple task. I shall return to where the attack was made. The cattle continued down the arroyo when last I saw them. It is probable they are still in the arroyo. Would it not be better to find them than to seek information from the Lunas?"

"That is true, but there is risk."

"There will be small danger. I have learned to move in the shadows and the brush with the silence of the coyote. I shall not be heard or seen."

Ryker glanced to Maria. It had grown so dark in the room he could scarcely make out her features. "This is agreeable with you?"

The woman was silent only briefly. "It is all right. You will take care, Miguelito?"

The boy's small shoulders squared. "I am not a child, Mama, and only a child would take a foolish risk. This was explained to me by Blas Armijo." He moved to the edge of the bed, an erect, sober young figure. "Trust this to me, my friend. When I return I shall have the

189

information you wish. Until later."

"Until later," Jake replied, and watched the boy slip from the room and disappear into the night.

XIX

The singing of the mockingbird somewhere in the yard aroused Ryker. He lay motionless on the narrow bed for several minutes, listening to the clear, trilling imitations of the bird while his mind gradually began to function. Maria had given him, besides doses of other kitchen-concocted remedies, something that had induced sleep. He had scarcely moved during the night. Now, as a result of such unbroken slumber, he was much stronger if slightly drugged.

Rolling to one side, he dropped his legs over the edge of the bed and sat up. His brain spun sickeningly and he hung motionless, irritably allowed the discomfort to pass. One thing, the myriad of aches that had belabored his battered frame were gone, and that was some relief.

He heard voices. They were coming from the yard. He started to rise, go there, but at that moment Maria entered the room. She gave him a quick, smiling glance, wheeled and returned to the kitchen to reappear shortly with a cup of steaming, thick chocolate.

The favored hot drink of the Mexican people was no novelty to him. Old Cocinero had brewed it regularly; still did, he supposed, although the cowhands as a rule preferred black coffee. Jake accepted the cup gratefully, nodded his thanks to her and took a deep swallow.

"You are much better," she commented, folding her hands together under the apron she was wearing.

He managed a grin. "You have good medicine. I am the same as well."

"There will still be a weakness. Another day, perhaps."

"I cannot wait another day," Ryker said, draining the cup and passing it back to her. "Has Miguel come?"

"Oh yes, by midnight. He found the cattle."

Jake Ryker straightened abruptly, then settled back slowly as pain smashed through his head. Reaching up he brushed the sweat that had gathered on his brow, swore under his breath.

Maria smiled sympathetically, creating the picture of a wise, dusky-skinned Madonna. "I have food prepared. After you have eaten doubtless you will feel much better."

"Likely, but first I must hear of my cattle. Where is Miguel? I would speak with him."

Maria shook her head. "He watches your herd and will return late in the day. He has told me the things you wish to know."

"Good. Tell me."

"After you have taken food," she replied firmly, and went into the kitchen.

When the meal, one of corn, slices of stewed chicken, tortillas and more chocolate, was over, Jake waited impatiently for Maria to clear away the dishes and return. When she did, he was on his feet, moving nervously but slowly about.

"Where did they take the cattle?" he asked before she could seat herself on the bench placed near the window.

"A short distance from where the attack was made, so Miguel said. In a place where Apache Wash is wide. The men believe you have been killed, and there is no necessity to drive the herd farther."

"They saw the Luna brothers ride away —"

"They fear nothing from them. They make a joke of their flight. Miguel heard one of the bandits say that both were so filled with dread that likely they have gone to Mexico."

"They will learn they are mistaken in many things," Ryker murmured grimly. "How many bandits are there? Was it mentioned by Miguel?"

"Four, although he said there was talk of another man to come. Also they expect to meet with yet a different man from Abilene for the purpose of selling him your cattle."

That was it then — rustlers and nothing more. He had successfully slipped by Teague's riders only to come up against a gang of rustlers.

"This buyer, was it said when he would come?"

"Nothing of such was said. Likely it will be tomorrow or perhaps the day that follows."

Taking into consideration the distances involved, that would be his guess, too. It didn't leave much time to make plans and act. Ryker plucked at his chin. What the hell could he do? He just couldn't stand by and let the outlaws get away with the herd, cattle that meant life or death for the Circle R.

Should he return to Medford's, seek the rancher's help? He'd not get it, he realized in the next breath. Not that the man wouldn't sympathize with his problem, but he had his hands full trying to hold his place together under the pressure of Bill Teague's steady aggression.

He could forget trying to recruit aid from the men in Polvareda. There'd be few, if any, guns around, and he doubted if there were any more experienced hands such as Blas Armijo available. Too, the villagers, aware of the *vaquero's* death and that the Luna brothers had fled for their lives, would want no part of his troubles.

He had the day to come up with something, some plan. One day in which to fully recover his strength, get back on his feet and have a program worked out that would enable him to recover the stock. One day. . . .

The way it shaped up, he reckoned there was little else he could do but wait out the sun. He would have to stall until dark to have his look at the place where the cattle were being held; he should hold off for Miguel, see if there had been any changes. Too, he doubted if he'd be up to a hard ride in the heat right then, regardless of how much he would like to act.

Moving to the bed, he sat down. Maria, who had remained silent on the bench during the time he was pacing back and forth, rose and went into the kitchen where she began making preparations for the day.

There was no stove in the room, only a corner fireplace in which pots could be suspended or a grill of iron bars placed above the flames. Everything was meticulously clean. Even the dirt floor, which was a dustless surface made so by countless sprinklings of water and painstaking sweeping. It was as hard as if made of oak planks.

The little nag of worry that had come to his mind earlier concerning the safety of Maria and Miguel should it become known they had befriended him again rose in Jake Ryker's mind. But he knew the matter should not be broached directly to the woman.

"It is a good home you and Miguel have," he said, rising and starting again to prowl.

"It belonged to the family of my husband. It was given to us on the day of our marriage," Maria replied, coming back into the room. She gazed wistfully about. "There was much happiness here until —"

Jake, halted by the window, nodded understandingly when she hesitated. "Until your husband was lost. How did that happen?"

"He was slain by a man."

"By an American?"

"By a *gringo*. An incident near the store. One of little importance in itself. Words were passed concerning the Mexican people. My husband refused the insult and made a reply."

"An act of courage."

"Yes, but the man drew his pistol and killed him."

"Was your husband armed?"

"No. Long ago we learned it is unwise to carry weapons. Only those like Blas Armijo have done so."

"Such was murder. Is there no lawman close by?"

Maria's short laugh was dry with scorn. "The law is not for my people, only for the Americans and the *gringos*."

Ryker looked at her curiously. "You speak of the Americans and the *gringos* as if different. Is not a *gringo* an American?"

"There is difference," she answered with a shrug. "Both are Americans, just as you are an American. But you are not a *gringo*. That is a word reserved for those who have no understanding or respect for our ways or our persons. They are those who would treat us as if we were of less importance than the lowliest dog. Those we call Americans, as yourself, look upon us as equals, as a people having rights and entitled to be

197

accorded and judged as Americans would their own race."

It was a long speech and it had brought color to Maria Calderon's cheeks — an angry flush. She looked away.

"I see," Ryker murmured. "Many times I have wondered about the term. I now understand. I am sorry about your husband. Words are of small solace, I know, and I fear I may have brought new troubles upon you."

Maria again moved her shoulders. "If it comes, it will come. There is little that can be done to avoid trouble, even less to meet it. We do not live, we exist from day to day. When there is happiness, it is possible to do so without thought. But when —" Her voice trailed off as she rose abruptly and went into the kitchen.

"It is best that you sleep," she called back. "By the coming of night your strength will be with you. Then you can do what must be done."

Jake nodded, stretched out on the padded bunk. "True, it is best, but if the boy comes will you call me?"

"I shall do so," Maria promised, and busied herself at her chores.

XX

Near the end of the day Miguel Calderon rode in. He had been gone since early morning, had spent the hours hiding in the brush watching over the herd and the rustlers. There had been no change, he told Ryker.

Jake, fit once more, thanks to Maria's periodic medications and his own vitality, had awaited the boy's return anxiously. Now, with the evening meal over, his patience was again being taxed as he stalled out the minutes until darkness settled over the land. It was a good two hour ride to where the cattle were, the boy had informed him, but since it was across open country they would have to use extreme care in approaching.

Miguel was right he saw, when a while later they cut out of the wash, circled west and came to a halt on a low butte from which they could see the herd. Only a thin screen of chamiso and plume prevented their being seen by the rustlers.

The raiders had brought the cattle to a

halt where the arroyo had flattened out into a shallow swale. There was little there for the herd to graze on, and it was immediately evident to Jake Ryker that the men would have difficulty holding the steers for any length of time. With no water and only scattered clumps of bunch grass the stock would have to be moved in the next day or so.

"There are four bandits," Miguel said, pointing to the small campfires, placed one at each side of the hollow. "They do not rest but ride back and forth. I believe they fear for something."

Ryker did not doubt it. The rustlers probably realized they had a powder keg with a lit fuse on their hands. "It is something they must do," he said. "Unless the cattle are kept quiet they will stampede. They are in a bad mood."

As he spoke he was watching the riders nearest the embankment. They had paused by the fire, dismounted. One was gathering more of the dry wood strewn about and replenishing the dwindling flames. Jake wished it were possible to work in closer, listen to what was being said. He might then get some idea of their plans and come up with a thought of his own as to how he could recover the stolen beef.

"Another man comes."

Miguel's low warning brought him around. He turned his head, saw a rider loping in from the east. There was something familiar in the way he sat his saddle, and Ryker had the feeling he had met the man before. But in the darkness, only partly relieved by a moon harried by scudding clouds, and because of the distance that separated them, he could distinguish nothing clearly.

The newcomer pulled up to the fire where the outlaws had paused. Without dismounting, he conversed with the pair for several minutes and then, wheeling around, doubled back over the trail he had just traveled.

He had brought a message of some sort to the rustlers, Jake concluded. Probably word as to when the buyer from Abilene could be expected. Ryker rubbed at his jaw uneasily. Whatever he planned to do must be done soon, and with the cattle growing more restless and unmanageable with each passing hour, they would become increasingly difficult to handle.

Again he considered the idea of riding to the Box M and asking Medford for help — and once more dismissed the suggestion, knowing the rancher would be compelled

201

to refuse because of his own problems. Too, it would be a fatal mistake; Teague's men, keeping close watch over Medford and his crew, would see Box M riders pulling out and follow. Thus they would be led to the herd, and it would be for Jake Ryker just a matter of jumping from the kettle into the pot.

But with no help how could he expect to recover three hundred thirsting, hungering steers primed for a stampede at the slightest provocation?

That was it!

The answer to his self-imposed question came in a single flash, like a beam of sunlight breaking suddenly through an overcast sky. Touching Miguel's arm, he drew back, returned to where they had tethered the horses.

"Do you know, young friend, is there a town near here on the New Mexico side of the border?"

Miguel pursed his lips, drew his brows together. "Yes, a place that is called Llano. I have not been there, however."

"Do you know where it lies from here?"

The boy stared off into the pale night. "I am not certain, but I believe it is to the north. I have heard the men speak of it. You will go there?"

"Not for help. There would be no point in such. I could not ask others to assume my trouble and thus endanger their lives. Already Blas Armijo is dead, and the Luna brothers live in fear for their lives because of me. And you —"

"I do not fear."

"I know, and I shall not permit it to come to you and your mother. As well we return to your house now. I have a plan to consider deeply."

They mounted, cut off through the scattered brush to where they were again in the more easily crossed arroyo.

"This plan," Miguel said in a tentative voice, "does it include me?"

"I am afraid not. The danger of your getting hurt will be too great."

"No harm has come to me yet. May I ask what is this plan?"

"A simple one. I shall stampede the cattle in the direction of New Mexico. From what I was told the border is but a space of ten miles, even less. If I am able to get the cattle to run that far, there is a good possibility I can recover them. This will be more true if there is a town where a lawman can be found."

"I see," Miguel said gravely. "I do not know if there is a sheriff in Llano or not. It is a larger village than Polvareda, so I have heard. Perhaps my mother will provide the answer."

Ryker hoped Maria Calderon would be able to tell him the location of the town as well. Driving the cattle straight for it would be almost as important as finding a lawman to whom he could show his papers for the herd and ask protection from the rustlers.

"It will be difficult for you alone to cause a stampede," Miguel continued in that serious, old man way of his. "There are four bandits, five if the one we saw this night returns. Must you not deal with them before you can get the cattle to run away?"

Ryker nodded. "It is a problem I must solve," he admitted.

"In that case I can be of help."

Jake smiled at the boy in the half-dark. "I am sorry, young friend, but I must decline the offer. As I have said, this time the danger will be far too great."

"And as I have said, also, no harm has come to me before, for I have taken care."

"This will be different. There will be shooting."

"Was there not shooting before?"

"Yes, and a good man was slain. I cannot

permit you to be exposed to such."

The boy fell silent for a time, then: "Will you again leave the question of this to my mother?"

Jake Ryker swore softly. Winning an argument from Miguel was a difficult task. There was always a stubborn logic to his way of thinking that was not easy to get around.

"Very well, it shall be your mother's decision. I shall tell her of what I plan, also of a new thought that has come to me concerning the two of you. Then we will see what she decides."

XXI

A stillness lay between the man Ryker and the boy Miguel as they rode into Polvareda. They entered by a back way, following a path that took them through fields of maize, small gardens of chili and ripening squash and melons, along a line of sun-grayed sheds and brush. Jake felt it was a necessary precaution since there was still the possibility the outlaws, having failed to find his body, could be keeping a watch on the village.

Dismounting, Miguel took the reins of the horses and said, "I shall care for the animals," and led them off to the lean-to that had been erected by him beneath a tree in the rear where it could not be easily noted.

Jake, feeling a bit shaky from the long ride, nodded, made his way to the house. Maria was waiting in the doorway and motioned him to a chair at a table where she had hot chocolate and tasty *galletas* ready.

"You are not well," she said, accusing him with her tone. "It was too soon for you

206

to have made such a journey."

"I am all right," he replied, impatient with himself. He took a deep swallow of the thick, sweet drink, wishing again it was black coffee, or a good belt of straight whiskey. But it helped, and he sighed, leaned back in the chair.

"You have seen your cattle?"

He nodded, feeling the place in his arm where Lenny Gault's bullet had cut its path. The wound it had etched ached dully.

"They are in Apache Wash as Miguel has said. Four men guard them. While we watched a fifth outlaw came with a message. I believe it was regarding the buyer they are expecting."

Maria refilled his cup from the earthenware pot. "You will be able to recover the herd?"

"I must try," he said simply, and glanced to Miguel, just entering the doorway.

The boy took his place at the table solemnly, greeting his mother with only his eyes, and took up his cup of chocolate. Barely sipping it, he looked at Ryker.

"You have asked her?"

Jake Ryker shook his head. "I wished you to be here so that you might hear all that was said."

He lowered his eyes. "Thank you."

Maria's attention sharpened. "What is it I am to be asked that is so important?"

Ryker folded his arms across his chest. "I have a plan to recover my cattle. Tomorrow morning I shall attempt it. But first there is another matter I must speak of."

He paused, glanced around the small room. "This house — would it be difficult for you to leave it?"

Maria frowned. "I — I am not certain of your meaning. In truth, leaving this house has never entered my mind."

"You spoke once of being happy here as if it were no longer possible."

The woman shrugged. "Happiness of one sort. There is another that comes of being a mother with a fine son. I have him with me and there is happiness in that."

"I understand."

The boy was staring at him intently. "What is it you would say?"

Ryker shifted on his chair. He wished he could speak in English rather than in the stiffly precise Spanish tongue; it would be much easier to express what he had in his mind.

"I do not think it is good that you remain here. I fear the outlaws will find that you have helped me after I have gone and take revenge. Therefore, I ask you to come with me to the ranch of my brother and me, and make it your home."

Miguel's eyes brightened. Maria at once became thoughtful.

"Why?"

"The reason has been given, the important one. I fear for you. Also, Miguel is deserving of more than he can receive here in Polvareda. I would give him the opportunity to work, to become a man. I would help him — and you."

She studied him coolly. "What would I do at this ranch of yours?"

He knew what she was thinking and shook his head. "Your person would be inviolate," he replied, stumbling for the proper word. "No harm would ever befall you. I have not said this but my brother has been injured. He can no longer walk. If I wish it he and his wife will move into the town and the ranch will be in my charge. It is no great ranch, only a small one with a few men — mostly elderly."

"I would thus be cook and housekeeper for you?"

"Something of that nature. There is now a cook, however, a Mexican we call Cocinero. You could help him if you

209

wished, or decline. It would not matter."

"I see."

"It would be a good life for you and the boy. I will tell you that it was in my mind not to stay there once I had returned with the cattle. Now I find that I have different feelings, ones I cannot exactly explain to myself."

Jake Ryker paused seemingly puzzled and not a little surprised at what he was saying. "Since I have met you and Miguel there is a change. My acquaintance with you has opened my eyes to — to the belief that in this life there are more worthwhile matters than the waywardness that I felt was freedom."

Again he was stumbling for proper words, and a fine beading of sweat had appeared on his forehead.

"Miguel would learn the business of cattle raising. Perhaps one day he could have a ranch of his own. If such was not his desire, there would always be a job for him with me."

Maria nodded slowly. "What of your brother and his wife? Would they agree to this arrangement?"

"It would not be for them to say since they will be living in the town. However, they would welcome you."

It was likely Tom would approve of the idea; probably Callie would not. It didn't matter. He would see to their comfort and guarantee that they would never want for anything.

"Such is what I have often dreamed of . . ."

Miguel's voice came to him. He glanced up. The boy was staring at his mother, eyes aglow.

"We would live in a fine house as we have often hoped, be proud and honored."

Maria smiled softly. "I know, Miguelito, but it is hard to leave this house of your father's, the people who are our friends."

"We could make new friends, better friends — ones who would not fail us as they did my father!"

Ryker pushed back his chair. "I shall go outside if you wish to discuss the matter."

"There is no need," Maria replied. "It is what Miguel wishes, therefore it is what I also wish. There is this small problem."

"Problem?"

"In this house, humble as it is, there are a few things that I will wish to keep. They are family possessions that one day should be the property of Miguel's wife, when such comes to pass."

"It will be possible to take them."

"How can it be done? On a saddle —"

"Is there someone in the village who will lend or perhaps sell to me a wagon and horse?"

"Procopio Mondragon — he has a small carriage that can be drawn by one horse," Miguel said quickly. "He no longer has use for either. The vehicle is what you call a — a board."

"Buckboard?"

"Yes, that is the name!"

"It will do fine. Then it is agreed? In the morning we will see this Procopio Mondragon, buy or borrow from him the horse and buckboard. You will load up the things you wish to keep. You will take food and water for at least three days' journey. I shall furnish you with a map showing you how my ranch is to be found."

"You will not accompany us?"

"No, I shall be with the cattle."

"But if you do not return, what of your brother and his wife? We shall be strangers."

"They will welcome you as if I were there — which I shall be. I will give you a letter telling them of what I had planned. Regardless you will have a home."

Maria shrugged. "I do not know . . . It would not be the same."

"For Miguel it would and for you, also. My brother requires great care on the part of his wife. You would be of aid and comfort to her."

"I would not wish us to be a burden because of a kindness given."

"You would not be. Then it is arranged?"

"It is agreed."

"Good. I shall make my plans for recovering the herd and go to the wash after I see that you and Miguel are on the way."

Maria stared thoughtfully at her folded hands. "This has occurred to me; how can you, one man, take the cattle from four, perhaps five, outlaws?"

"By allowing the cattle to do it for me. Do you have a blanket or a large piece of cloth that I may have?"

"A blanket, yes. How can it help?"

"The steers are hungry and thirst badly. In the morning I plan to go where they are being held. I shall avoid the rustlers and at any opportunity, stampede the animals. Using the blanket and my pistol, it will not be a difficult task with the cattle in such nervous condition. I shall come at them from the east side, thus forcing them to run to the west and the New Mexico border."

213

Maria's lips had parted into a small, admiring smile. "I understand. But will not these bandits try to prevent you from frightening the herd?"

"It will be necessary to slip by them unnoticed until the stampede has begun," he admitted.

"And such will be possible only with my help," Miguel said. "I shall go with him, Mama."

Maria Calderon's mouth tightened at the boy's pronouncement. A paleness came into her cheeks. "Are you not to come with me in the wagon? Is that not the plan?"

"He is our good friend, this man called Ryker," Miguel said stubbornly. "It would be wrong to let him face so difficult a task unaided. My father would have said so. Blas Armijo would also have said so. You will start with the wagon. After the cattle have begun the running and are safe in New Mexico, I shall hurry and join you."

Maria, features grave, shifted her eyes to Jake. "This is your wish?"

"I cannot deny that his help would be welcome to me, but I will not ask him to give it unless you permit him to do so. There is small doubt that there will be considerable danger."

Face sober, the boy watched his mother.

214

Only his pleading eyes betrayed the hope that surged within him.

"He is all I have, all that remains of love, of a fine man —"

"That I have realized. Miguel and I agreed that it would be your decision. If you do not wish it to be, the matter will end. Either way, it does not alter our other plans."

Maria rose, walked slowly to the doorway and gazed off into the silvery night. Something disturbed the chickens in their nearby pen of woven willow reeds. There was a brief flurry of clucking, then quiet.

"He is truly not a man, only a small boy —"

"With a man's good sense of responsibility and duty to you."

"This I know. Very well, to refuse would be great hurt to him. He shall go with you, but I shall also come. It is possible I can help with the cattle in some way. Also, there is the matter of cooking during the journey. Such tasks will be my lot."

Ryker's shoulders stiffened. "That is not wise."

A stubbornness came into Maria Calderon's features. Her lips set themselves firmly, formed a tight bow. "Only in this way shall I agree."

215

Jake Ryker shrugged, turned to the boy. "I am sorry, young friend, but I cannot permit —"

"There is no place for a woman, Mama!" Miguel cried, ignoring Jake. "This you must understand!"

"I shall not be in the way but remain in the distance, if such pleases you. Then, when it is all over, I would join you."

The boy turned to Ryker. In the yellow, flickering flare of the candles placed on the table, his face reflected worry and uncertainty. Jake smiled, dropped a hand on his shoulder.

"It is all right," he said and turned his attention to Maria. "You will keep far from us and the herd until we are safely in New Mexico. Then we will meet. This is thoroughly understood?"

"It is understood," Maria replied, also smiling.

XXII

It was Maria who went to deal with old Procopio Mondragon. Deciding to prepare for the trip immediately, and fearing to have Ryker in the open where he might be seen by one of the outlaws should they be keeping an eye on the village, she assumed the task of acquiring the horse and buckboard which was to furnish transportation for her and her belongings to New Mexico.

She did well, bargaining away those pieces of household furniture and other items she did not wish to keep, along with the chickens, two pigs and a small hoard of preserved fruit and vegetables that she had set aside for the winter months. When she had finished it was necessary for Jake to hand over only five silver dollars of his dwindling funds to the elderly Mexican.

They slept but little in the few remaining hours of the night and were up long before first light. Maria prepared a final breakfast, extending her cooking activities at that time to include food that was to be carried for use during the remainder of the day.

Then, as the sun broke over the foothills to the east, the tiny cavalcade moved out, careful to keep the trees and brush between them and the settlement so as not to be observed. They traveled together for the first few miles, eventually separating, Maria continuing due west, Jake and the boy slanting off toward the south.

Looking back over his shoulder at the buckboard with its solitary passenger as it disappeared beyond a rise, Miguel turned an anxious face to Ryker.

"She will be safe, is that not true?"

Jake nodded. "Your mother is a very wise woman, young friend. She knows well what she does. We need have no fear for her."

The boy looked at him with steady intent. "Do you not also believe that my mother is very beautiful?"

Jake Ryker rubbed at his stubble of beard. He'd not shaved for several days now and the bristles were beginning to be a bother.

"There is no doubt of that."

"A wise and beautiful woman," Miguel murmured, settling back. "A man who would take her for his wife would indeed be most fortunate."

Ryker cast a wondering glance at the boy, but Miguel's eyes were off in the distance, blandly innocent. Jake grinned wryly, swore under his breath. There were times when he was certain Miguel was older than he thought.

The morning was clear, already warm as they rode steadily on. They followed a route somewhat east of Apache Wash, planning to come in, as Ryker had determined earlier, on the flank of the herd. If the stampede succeeded and the cattle reacted as expected, the herd should take flight in the opposite direction: a course that would carry them out of Texas into its adjacent neighbor, New Mexico.

Jake looked again to Miguel. The boy's features were smooth, a light brown in the strong light. A dreaminess filled his eyes, and Ryker knew he was living and enjoying those first moments of being a man in a man's world. He would be a credit to his mother and to the Circle R.

"We are near," the boy said a time later, slowing his pony and pointing off to his right. "The brush that looks to be a fence grows along the rim of the arroyo."

Ryker pulled up. They were still a considerable distance from the herd, he thought, but he could not be sure. He'd been through there only once, and that at night.

"The herd, is it also near?"

"A distance yet, I believe. Perhaps a mile."

Jake accepted the boy's judgment without question. Swinging the chestnut to the left and down into a narrow gully, he resumed the wide circuit. When they had covered what he considered the necessary length, he once again halted, checked now by the faint bawling of cattle. He nodded in satisfaction. They were directly opposite the herd.

He could see nothing of the steers, however, nor of the men, hopefully still no more than four in number. The ground rose in a fair swell before them and clumps of brush and sun-scoured weeds blocked the openness of the country. He motioned to the boy.

"We will move toward the cattle. It is necessary you keep the chamiso and such growth in front of you at all times so that you will not be seen by the outlaws. Since we cannot see them, it is not possible to know of their exact positions."

Miguel said, "I understand. The embankment is high on this side of the arroyo. It will protect us . . . Is that not smoke?"

Jake looked quickly to where Miguel

indicated, somewhat to their right and above the wash. A thin streamer of black was twisting lazily up into the empty sky.

"That'll be them, sure'n hell," he muttered in English, and then bucked his head at the boy. "They have made a fire for cooking. We are in a good place."

He touched the gelding with his rowels, sent him moving on. Immediately he slowed, beckoned to Miguel. "Keep to my left hand," he directed, and resumed the slow, careful advance. If shooting developed unexpectedly, he wanted to be in between the boy and the rustlers.

Miguel moved into position, not questioning the order, likely giving it no thought. They pressed on, taking advantage of the scarce brush, the scattered junipers, the minor gullies and washes that broke the flatness of the land.

The sounds of the cattle grew louder, and from the timbre and frenzied quality of the bawling, Jake realized the animals were in a bad frame of mind, needed but little to send them into a wild flight.

He would have no difficulty in starting the stampede; the problem would be getting in near enough to the steers without being seen by the outlaws. If he began the stampede attempt while still at a distance,

221

the cattle could break and head into the wrong direction — or worse yet, split into several bunches each having its own idea of where to go.

The chestnut broke out of a low swale, climbed a short grade and halted as Ryker pulled him in sharply. They had reached the edge of Apache Wash. The cattle were a quarter mile ahead on the farther side of the flat and sandy stretch of open ground. A few hundred yards to the right Jake saw the rustlers.

There were still four of them. This was small consolation, however; the instant he and Miguel left the embankment and started across the flat for the herd, they would be seen. Rifles would open up and they would both go down before they were well started.

Wheeling the gelding about, Ryker dropped back into the swale. Dismounting, he tied the gelding to a scrub, motioned for the boy to do likewise. Keeping low, he returned to the edge of the arroyo.

Miguel, at his side, eyes on the herd, murmured quietly. "It is a far distance to the cattle."

"Much too far," Ryker agreed. "And it is not possible to race a bullet and win even on the fastest horse."

222

"That is true. Also there are no places in which to hide. Would it not be wise to circle and approach from the other side? Or perhaps, from below?"

"I am afraid to do so. The cattle will take fright easily. If we do not go at them from this side, it is hard to guess what they will do. My plan to recover the steers depends upon driving them into New Mexico."

"This I know. But if it is not possible —"

"Got to make it possible, dammit all!" Ryker declared, lapsing into more vigorous English. "Come this far, by God I'm not quitting now!"

"Pardon?"

Jake glanced at the boy, shrugged. "It was nothing. I said only that a way must be found. If the bandits could be attracted to something, persuaded to leave only long enough for us to go forward with the blanket and start the stampede, we would have —"

Jake Ryker's words faded into silence. A frown crossed his face as he saw motion at the edge of the arroyo some distance beyond the outlaws, crouched now about their fire drinking coffee.

A buckboard . . . A solitary occupant. Ryker strained for a better look while fear toyed with him. It couldn't be Maria. She

223

was supposed to cross the wash miles to the north. Yet, it looked like her. If so, how could she have gotten so far off course?

It had been no error on her part but a deliberate move; he realized that even as he recognized her for certain. She had perceived the night before his need to draw the outlaw's attention to permit him and Miguel to work in close to the cattle; she was simply making it possible.

He saw her stand up in the buckboard, survey the broad, sandy wash as if searching for a place to cross. The bright flash of a colored petticoat, the sharp contrast of her snow white shirtwaist and black dress was distinct.

One of the outlaws came to his feet abruptly, face turned to her. He looked down, said something to his companions. They rose also, and for a long minute all four stood and stared as if in disbelief. Then, suddenly, they tossed away their tin cups and wheeled to their horses. Leaping to the saddle, all raced off for the buckboard with its tempting woman occupant.

"It is your mother," Ryker said, drawing the boy's attention to the departing riders. "She makes it possible for us to start the stampede."

At once Miguel's face showed alarm. "Will they not harm her?"

"Not if we act quickly," Ryker said leaping to his feet. Wheeling, he hurried to where the horses waited. Miguel followed at his heels.

Mounting, Ryker pulled the blanket Maria had given him from his saddlebags, ripped off a third of it and tossed it to the boy.

"Do not wave the cloth until we are near. I shall give the signal."

Miguel nodded, but his gaze was to the north — to the buckboard.

"Do not worry," Jake reassured him. "When the outlaws see us they will halt and return instantly. Your mother will be forgotten. Come — there is little time to lose!"

Jamming spurs into the chestnut's flanks, he sent the big horse lunging out of the swale, across the narrow ridge and into the arroyo.

XXIII

Ryker restrained the gelding, held him to an easy lope, fearing that too fast an approach would spook the cattle, cause them to break and run too soon. He threw a glance after the four men rushing toward Maria Calderon. They had not noticed Miguel and him as yet, being too intent on the woman. With a little more luck his timing should prove to be perfect.

A frown crossed his features; he'd congratulated himself too soon. Another rider had appeared on the flat, was loping steadily toward the wash. The fifth outlaw again. A grim smile pulled at Jake's lips. Four to one odds weren't bad enough, it seemed — they had to go to five! But there was nothing to be done about it. Jaw set, he rode on, careful but without deviation.

The cattle were bawling noisily, shifting restlessly about in small bunches. He didn't know if the rustlers realized it or not, but chances were better than good that they'd be unable to hold the herd in the wash much longer — even if he wasn't

226

about to start them off on a wild run. It could be that the buyer from Abilene and his drovers were due to arrive that morning and take over, and such could be the reason for their indifference. One thing sure, the Abilene cattle broker had made a long ride for nothing, regardless of how matters turned out.

Jake looked ahead. The herd was near. Many of the steers had faced about, and heads hung low, were watching Miguel and him with suspicious eyes. He slowed the chestnut. It would be unwise to press in too close. Looking to the boy, he raised his arm as a signal.

"Use your cloth but take care! Do not let your horse get in front of the steers!"

At once Miguel let out a piercing screech and taking the oblong of cloth tucked under his arm, began to wave it back and forth.

Ryker, unfurling his piece of the blanket in the same moment, shouted, drove spurs into the gelding, and sent him thundering toward the line of steers.

The lead animals broke, flung themselves about, horns clacking loudly as they came in contact with the steers behind them. There was a quick boiling up of dust, a surge of sound, and then in a solid

227

mass of flowing color the herd began to move toward the west bank of the broad arroyo.

The steers had turned fast and headed due west as he had hoped. Now, if Miguel could keep them running in a straight line — he glanced toward the boy. The youngster was bent low on his pony, mouth wide as he yelled, while he continued to use the strip of blanket. Mindful of the warning Jake had given him, he was staying back from the herd and a bit to the side. His mere presence there should keep the herd from swinging off —

The faint crack of pistols lifted above the drum of pounding hooves. Ryker instantly swung his attention to the upper end of the arroyo. The outlaws were returning. He could barely see them through the thickening dust haze, strung out in an uneven line as they raced toward the herd. Their fifth member was midway into the wash, angling in to intercept and join them.

Jake raised himself slightly in his stirrups, strained to catch a glimpse of Maria. There was no sign of her, and worry began to tag at his mind. She should be crossing the arroyo unless the outlaws, out of spite —

More gunshots echoed through the

228

choking air. Ryker grinned tautly. The rustlers were only helping by using their weapons. The shooting served only to further frighten the cattle, caused them to increase their speed. But they weren't thinking of the cattle, he knew.

Weapon in hand, he veered to the right, still hoping to see Maria and the buckboard. Gusts of dust swept against him and he reached for his bandana, drew it up over his mouth and nose. In almost that identical instant one of the outlaws appeared directly ahead. He fired hastily.

The bullet went wide of its target, but the rustler swung off, pointing for the denser haze. Jake threw a second shot at the man and cut back toward the tail of the hard-running herd. A solid wall of yellow now lay all about him, dry, choking and blinding — but he was grateful for it. The pall was a curtain shutting off the outside world and the five men endeavoring to close in on him.

He swiped at the sweat caking dust on his face and clogging his eyes. The cattle were now out of the wash, were pounding across the long mesa that lay to the west. They showed no indication yet of slowing. Held for so many hours without water and ample forage, they were wild to run, to expend their nervousness and temper.

Keeping a sharp watch on his rear where he figured the outlaws were most likely to appear, Ryker looked about, hopeful of a glimpse of Miguel. He saw him a moment later. The boy was holding his position, still shouting and waving his flag. Satisfaction pushed through Jake as he let the gelding fall back. It was going to be easier than he'd thought; the cattle were continuing in a straight line and the possibility the rustlers were giving up and moving off was growing. He'd seen no more of them.

But Maria . . .

He spurred the chestnut on toward the center rear of the herd where he planned to ride, slicing diagonally across its wake until he reached the flank. Maria should be somewhere on the flat to the north unless something had happened back in the arroyo.

Relief flowed through him as he caught sight of her, when he emerged from the film of dust. She was driving the buckboard parallel to the cattle, keeping pace as best she could at a distance of only a hundred yards or so. She had tied what appeared to be her white petticoat to the back of the vehicle's seat; it was flapping vigorously as the buckboard bounced along at top speed.

The ease that had slipped over him upon seeing her safe changed then to anger. She had ignored his instructions to stay clear of the herd and take no risks. Muttering an oath, Jake Ryker spurred to catch up. She saw him coming, turned a dust-smeared face to him.

"Pull away!" he shouted, motioning her off with his hand.

She shook her head, continued her course alongside the running cattle. Her position there was the reason the herd was maintaining its direct line of flight, he knew. And with Miguel on the opposite flank and him crowding from the rear, the stampeding steers were doing exactly as he wished.

But he didn't like the thought of her exposing herself to such danger. If the thundering cattle for some reason cut north, she would have a difficult time getting out of their path — if she could at all.

"Too close!" he yelled, and again waved at her to move away.

Maria only smiled. She recognized the need for having someone flanking the herd on that side, accepted the responsibility. Ryker swore again. He had quite a pair on his hands — Maria Calderon and her son

Miguel! But that didn't lessen the worry plaguing him. She must be made to realize, to understand —

He saw her raise her arm, point excitedly toward the rear of the herd. He looked quickly. Two riders were cutting through the dust for the opposite side.

"Miguel!" Maria screamed at him.

He caught the fear in her voice even as it welled through him, and instantly swung away, roweling the chestnut cruelly as he bore straight for the pair. They had evidently spotted the boy at his key position, were intending to drive him off and turn the herd . . . They hadn't given up on the cattle after all.

Low on the gelding's outstretched neck, Ryker leveled his pistol at the dim figures coming in on the left. They were yet unaware of his presence, thanks to the swirling dust and the continuous thud of the running steers. They wouldn't be for long. Approaching on a course that would intercept them, they were bound to catch sight of him shortly and his advantage would be lost.

The outlaw slightly to the rear of his partner was the first to notice. He stiffened suddenly, surprised at Ryker's nearness. His arm swung up and he pressed off a shot. The report was a dry crack above the dull roar of the stampede. Jake felt the breath of the bullet as it whipped by his head.

He fired back as the first of the two looked over his shoulder: a dark-faced man whose whiskers were matted with sweat and dust. Ryker's bullet missed but his second shot found its mark. The outlaw jolted, clawed at his belly and wheeled off into the murk.

His companion opened up instantly. Ryker winced as a leaden slug ripped across his thigh, leaving a streak of red; as another slapped against the horn of his saddle, screamed into space.

Hunched low, steadying his right arm with his left hand while he allowed the chestnut to run free, he triggered his weapon again. The pistol bucked in his grasp. The rustler recoiled, sagged to one side as his horse rushed on.

Again Jake Ryker took deliberate aim. His bullet had gone true but evidently had struck no vital place. The man was still in the saddle, still slanting across to get at Miguel. He pressed off the trigger once more, swore savagely as the hammer came down on an empty cartridge.

Cursing, he let the chestnut slow as he

thumbed cartridges from his belt. He should have taken greater care, been mindful of the number of times he'd gotten off a shot. Never before had he been guilty of such laxity. What the hell was wrong with him? In his anxiety to look after Maria and Miguel he'd left himself wide open for a bullet.

Reloading, he spurred the gelding into a fast lope again, brushing at his eyes to clear his vision while he searched the gloom for the outlaw. The man was no longer visible but he could not have gotten far.

Abruptly Jake saw him. He was directly ahead. Beyond him the indistinct, smaller figure of Miguel Calderon was a blur in the haze, still bent over his straining little pony, switching his piece of flannel back and forth. The boy was unaware of the outlaw's presence, was intent on the job of keeping the steers running hard and straight.

Ryker brought up his gun, threw a shot at the outlaw to distract him. Instantly the man glanced around. He veered off, evidently taken by surprise by Jake's nearness. His own weapon came up, paused. Cool, Ryker once more steadied himself, squeezed off his pistol. The rustler folded to one side. His horse shied at the unexpected shift of weight on his back, cut sharply to the opposite direction. The outlaw fell to the ground, bounced limply like a rag doll, and lay still.

The firing attracted Miguel's attention. He twisted about, features smudged with dirt and sweat, choking and coughing from the spinning dust. Jake lifted a reassuring hand to him, swung away to resume his place at the rear of the herd.

The steers were slowing down, but they should be drawing near the New Mexico border. Another two or three miles, Jake reasoned, and all would be well. He'd let the stock run until they stopped of their own accord. Such should guarantee that they would be far out of Texas. One thing, there sure as hell had better be some water close; after a run like that he'd have some dead beef on his hands unless —

Three riders spurted suddenly from the bank of yellow to his left. Ryker's jaw sagged as he recognized the man in the lead — Max Cameron! The others were strangers.

All fired at him simultaneously. He threw a bullet at the one nearest, saw him buckle even as he felt the chestnut falter, start down. Grim, he got off a second shot as he struck the ground, rolled clear of the gelding's flailing hooves.

Cameron — Medford's own foreman! He was the one back of the raid. It all came to Jake in a flash. It had been Cameron who laid out the plan for him, who had picked the route the herd would follow; then he'd had the rustlers waiting in ambush to take over when the herd reached a certain point.

Anger swept Jake Ryker as the full import of the doublecross registered on his mind. Likely Cameron worked regularly with the gang of rustlers, made it possible for them to help themselves to Medford cattle whenever they wished. But more, he was responsible for the death of Blas Armijo, for the near loss of the herd which wasn't really safe yet, and for all the grief and worry and pain —

"Goddam you!" Ryker yelled, and bounded to his feet.

He went into a half crouch, fired from the hip. The outlaw riding in tight on Cameron's left, jerked, slid from his saddle. One booted foot caught in the stirrup and the suddenly frightened horse bolted, galloped off dragging the outlaw through the dust.

Cameron's bullet smashed into his leg,

spun him half about, drove him to one knee. Ryker cursed, took dead aim at the oncoming man. The foreman had been the fifth man, the one he and Miguel had seen ride up the night before, the one who had joined the gang moments before the stampede started. Jake had thought he looked familiar; he now knew why.

He squeezed off the shot. Cameron stiffened, drew himself rigidly erect. An instant later the Box M foreman's shying horse was upon Ryker. Its foreleg caught him against the shoulder, knocked him back. Something struck his head, a loose, swinging stirrup, he guessed; and then he went down hard.

XXIV

Dazed, Jake Ryker shook off the smothering cloud of breathless dark that sought to weigh him down, struggled back to his feet despite the searing pain in his leg from the outlaw's bullet. Dust was swirling about him in a blinding cloud. He could see nothing, no one. The hammering pound of the stampeding herd seemingly had grown fainter.

Hand gripping his pistol, he swiped at his eyes and lips with a forearm, staggered forward a step, halted. Max Cameron lay on the baked, churned earth before him. The outlaw's lifeless eyes stared upward as if endeavoring to penetrate the layers of drifting silt hanging over him. Beyond the foreman was a prone shape of another of the rustlers. He tried to remember, to figure; he'd accounted for all of the outlaws — he thought. But he wasn't sure. There could still be one, possibly two running loose trying to turn the herd, recover it.

If so, there was nothing he could do about it. He was alone with the dead. His

238

mind swung to Maria, to the boy Miguel. He hoped they were unhurt, alive . . . And the cattle. The sound of their running was now a low rumble fading into the distance. He grinned wearily, once more brushed at his mouth. That had worked out pretty good — if they continued to run. If not, then it had all been for nothing; the killings, the blood, the sweat and worry, perhaps even the lives of Maria and Miguel, and his own.

Holstering his pistol, he glanced around. It was as if he were a solitary survivor in a room, one with tan walls that lifted and fell, thickened and thinned, ones that were unsubstantial yet solidly closed him off from the remaining world.

But the pall was dissipating. A quietness was settling over the flat and the diminishing drum of the racing cattle had ceased. He wished he had a horse. He turned, went to one knee as the wounded leg failed to respond, drew himself upright once more. Cameron's horse should be close, or else that of the outlaw lying near him. He had to find one, get into the saddle, see that Maria and Miguel were all right, that the cattle were safe — and get that hole in his leg plugged up before he bled himself out.

A grating sound came to him, brought him up short. It was the slicing noise iron-tired wheels made when cutting through loose sand.

"Ryker!"

A sigh went through him as a tight grin stretched the corners of his mouth. It was Maria Calderon's voice.

"Here — over here!" he shouted back.

He hung motionless for a few seconds, striving to locate her position, masked from him by the restless wall of dust. Abruptly the horse and then the buckboard, with Maria standing erect and looking anxiously about, broke through.

"Ryker!" she called again, relief now in her tone as she caught sight of him.

He bucked his head, moved toward her. The wounded leg gave out once again. He went half down, recovered himself and struggled on to meet her.

"Had me worried," he mumbled, forgetting to speak in Spanish. "You and the boy — was afraid —"

She only smiled at him, and leaped to the ground. Taking him by the arm, she assisted him into the buckboard and onto the seat. Then, taking quick note of his wound, she ripped a strip of cloth from the petticoat yet hanging from the vehicle's

240

backrest, quickly and expertly bound up the injury.

He reached out as she finished, caught her by the wrist. "Miguel? He has not been harmed?"

She shook her head. "He is with the cattle. They have reached the place of water. There is a village."

Jake released her. Features knitted into a frown, he waited while she circled the buckboard and climbed up to sit beside him.

"The cattle — they are all right, too?" There was a thread of doubt in his voice as if he found it hard to believe.

She unwound the reins, nodded. "They run to where they reach the small lake of the wind pump. There they have stopped. A few are dead but not many." Maria paused, her smooth, dusty features serious. "Ryker — I — I —" She hesitated again, a curious look in her eyes. "It is that I do not know your other name. Only Ryker. To call out such —"

"Jake — Jacob," he said.

"Jacobo," she murmured, translating it into her own tongue. "Jacobo . . . It is a good name. Now it is possible for me to properly call you."

Ryker heaved a sigh of contentment, settled onto the seat as the buckboard rolled forward. It was finished. Except for the wound in his leg and a few steers lost, they had come through unscathed. A day or two's rest, and then the drive to the Circle R would be as nothing. He glanced at the woman beside him, smiled.

"Jake, Jacobo — you call me anything," he said in English. "Makes no difference what, long as you don't stop."

Maria turned to him, puzzled. "What is it you say?"

Ryker grinned again. He'd explain it later at a better time.

We hope you have enjoyed this Large Print book. Other Thorndike Press or Chivers Press Large Print books are available at your library or directly from the publishers.

For more information about current and upcoming titles, please call or write, without obligation, to:

Thorndike Press
P.O. Box 159
Thorndike, Maine 04986 USA
Tel. (800) 257-5157

OR

Chivers Press Limited
Windsor Bridge Road
Bath BA2 3AX
England
Tel. (0225) 335336

All our Large Print titles are designed for easy reading, and all our books are made to last.